The

Foreign

Endgame

SEAN SCOTT KERNS

This book is a work of fiction. Names, characters, places, and incidents either are products of the author's imagination or are used fictitiously. Any resemblance to actual events or locals, or persons, living or dead, is entirely coincidental.

Copyright © 2017 Sean Scott Kerns

ISBN: *0991054652*
ISBN-13:978-991054657

DEDICATION

For Ms. Yvonne, Sharon, Lara, Angela,

Michelle and Ethelle, great fans, friends,

and family. For all the women who have

a breast cancer testimony, thank you for

setting the example of how to be a

survivor.

CONTENTS

ACKNOWLEDGMENTS

A special thanks to my mom, Travis one and Travis two for being big influencers in my life, and my co-workers for their technical support. Another big thanks to my content editor, proofreader and mentor Clarissa.

1

Negotiations and Transitions

Life as parents agreed with both
Mychal and Richard. She loved watching
him be Carrigan's father. They were on the
same parenting accord except for a few
things, one of which included childcare.
The issue first came up in finding someone
to keep the baby for the annual university
gala. It was not going to be held at the
house for security reasons, so they needed a
sitter. Richard called an agency that sent a
couple of qualified candidates for them to
interview. They interviewed each person

and argued after every one. There was an elderly lady that Richard liked, but Mychal did not, mainly because of her perfume.

"That is not a reason," Richard defended his choice.

"Richard, with that much perfume, the baby might have an allergic reaction," she explained. "Besides, who comes to a job interview smelling like they live at the perfume counter in a department store? It was coming out of her skin. Hell, I think I need more than some coffee beans to get my sense of smell back. I need a bath after that interview."

"That was so wrong to say. But if you want someone to share your bath, I am volunteering," he grinned.

"I accept your volunteer application and will review it later," she teased then, returned to the subject, "That woman is a no."

They were running out of time for a

sitter which would have suited Mychal just fine. She had mixed feelings about leaving the baby with a stranger anyway. The answer to her dilemma came when Pedro arrived to bring the baby a gift his wife had bought in the market. Mychal thanked him and inquired whether his wife ever worked with children. His reply was that she cared for Richard's grandparents as they declined in age. Impulsively, she asked if he thought his wife would keep the baby sometimes. Pedro gave her a bashful grin and said, "For the woman who has made Señor Ricardo so happy, I will ask."

Richard was surprisingly pleased with his wife's attempt to find a nanny and smiled, "You have always had Pedro wrapped around your finger. Abeulita Carmen was good to my grandparents and will make a great nanny, if she agrees."

Another event that made Richard happy was Susanna returning to school. As promised, she sat out the summer semester then returned in the fall semester.

However, she changed her major from orchestra instruction to music therapy, which would mean she needed additional classes. She came to the house after dinner to talk with her older brother about her decision. He was watching the soccer game with Carrigan.

"*Hola Hermano.*"

"Hello yourself. What drags you away from Javier to visit us?" Richard teased.

"Oh, ha ha," she plucked her niece right out of his arms. The baby made no fuss moving to her aunt. "I wanted to see this adorable face and talk with you about changing my major."

Richard rolled his eyes, "To what now?"

Susanna frowned, "Why are you acting like that? I have not said or done anything to get that reaction."

"You sat out a semester."

"In all honesty Richard, that was not the end of the world. I took time off to refocus and went back this semester," she defended her actions.

"You also got engaged after dating a guy less than six months." He could not suppress his sarcasm. "And now you want to change your major to what underwater basket weaving?"

"If you are going to act like this, there is no need for me to talk to you!" Susanna rose to give the baby back. She stood a little too quickly, which startled the baby and made her cry.

Richard sighed and went to take the infant from his sister. He gave her a pacifier and placed the baby on his shoulder. Carrigan quieted down. "I'm sorry *hermana*. Whenever it comes to you and school, I just assume it is always going to be bad news. I guess I am still mentally mending from you taking the summer off to find yourself."

"You are still stuck on that? I thought you were over it," Susanna was annoyed.

"I thought I was too until you came in here tonight," he put Carrigan in her swing and started it. He turned to his sister and said, "Now you have my full attention. Tell me your plans."

Susanna was quite stunned at her brother's sudden mood change. She took a breath and said, "I want to change from orchestra instruction to music therapy."

Richard gave her an interested look and nodded as if to say 'tell me more'. Susanna continued, "I want to work with soldiers in therapy by teaching them music as a coping skill. I also want to work with teaching blind children how to play instruments."

Her brother was more than

captivated by this new development, "Please tell me how you decided on this kind of humanitarian work and do not leave out one detail."

For the next half hour Susanna told Richard how over the summer she and Javier went to concerts at various parks, as well as restaurants. One band that performed a few times was a group of veterans from America. They had been injured in combat which ended their military careers. While in rehabilitation they met, and found that each band member shared a love for music. Two members played in high school but had to relearn to play new instruments due to their injuries. They taught their friends to master the instruments they could no longer play.

The former drummer who lost a leg, taught his friend the drums then learned to play the trumpet. The guitar player that lost his vision learned to play the piano and became the lead vocalist. The more

Susanna talked about how inspiring these veterans were, the more Richard could not miss her excitement as her body language changed. She became animated, her eyes bright with passion and her voice rose.

When Susanna finished the story of how their music inspired her, her older brother was convinced that she was going to make helping people with music her life's work. While Richard always knew she had no real plans for the family business, he was impressed with how Susanna was turning her love for music into a great career. And she would have his full support.

"Richard are you paying attention?" Susanna snapped her fingers and jolted him out of his deep thoughts. "I asked what you thought of all of this?"

"I think it is a marvelous idea. One that I hope you open as a business," Richard replied.

"Really?" his sister was skeptical at his reaction.

"Really," he confirmed.

Susanna was silent for a minute and then said, "So I have your full support?"

"As long as you turn it into some kind of business venture; yes. It can be profit or non-profit. I do not care which or you can make it both," Richard smiled.

Finally, she smiled back, "Okay then. That was too easy. I have come accustomed to my life discussions with you being a full fight. It feels weird to have you agree for a change. You should have had a baby sooner because it has definitely softened you."

"We do not argue and fight," he put up his hand in an air quote. "And yes, being a parent has refocused my attention. You can thank my wife for that one. She pointed out that none of your decisions have led you to join a band of traveling vampire circus clowns, so I need to trust you. Those were my wife's exact words, vampire circus clowns."

"Well, I owe her big time. But Ricardo, why the questioning? Why the pushback on everything I want to try? What have I done to make you not trust me and my decisions?"

Richard sighed. What had she done indeed? After a pause he said, "Nothing. You have done nothing and I guess it is not really about you."

Confused she asked, "Then what is it?"

Looking at his daughter, he replied, "It is that everything was, no is, changing. Before Mychal moved here, I knew what my life was going to be. I was going to follow in papa's footsteps. I was going to run the shipping company, marry a beautiful woman, not Demitri, and have a family. You would be like Madrina and marry someone as wonderful as Uncle Rico and spend your days in the arts or something. We would probably have to take care of Tony for the next decade or until he found a younger woman to have kids with but never marry. Wild spirits never settle down."

Susanna was stunned, "Wow. You have or had a interesting, almost dismal view of our futures."

"Not dismal, just prearranged. Papa always talked to me about being the man of the family and that meant making decisions that were not always comfortable."
Richard smiled, "He loved mama, but was ever the dutiful husband and family man in everything. You remember all those events we attended because it was our family duty."

"I do. Not just recitals but any other university, municipal, business, and family event that we had to go to as the children of Rohas and Alejandra Garçia-Torrés," she wondered where this was going.

"You had to convince me to even participate in the university's foreign exchange program. You said we were living our lives like a theater production with everybody having a role to play."

Susanna reminded him, "I said we were living scripted lives from what the previous generation expected of us. Which is why I don't really spend time with Soledad and the rest of mama's cousins. Their aristocratic nature consumes their lives. I hate it."

"I know. Tony has always openly rebelled against that mentality. But you, you shunned it, but quietly. When Mychal showed up, it was like her arrival gave you a voice. Not only did I have to deal with the bold American who was stealing my heart, I also had to process my little sister coming out of her shell. The same little girl whose hair I braided and took to school was starting to act like her twin."

"I was not," she interrupted.

"Of course you were not, but in my mind there was no middle ground. All I could see was you becoming a female Tony, careless, wild, and giving the finger to what our parents built."

Susanna signaled her understanding with a sigh, "You felt like a little more of their dream was slipping away. But *hermano*, I was not even doing anything close to Tony. I watched him push your limits over the years. I stopped counting the number of times you called Uncle Rico for Tony's exploits. Court appearances, bar fights, or someone's husband paying the company a visit. I just wanted to go out and learn who I was."

"*No importa. Mi hermanita se fue.*" Richard looked at Carrigan who was dozing off. "Again, change is difficult for me."

"I know. It always has been. You are not losing me. We will be family forever. I love you and will always be your *hermanita.*" She turned to leave, "One more thing."

"Yes?"

"Don't you think it is time to get to know Javier? It seems you still have some kind of hang-up about my relationship from the first comment you made."

Her question threw Richard off at first, "What do you mean? I have been more than cordial to your boyfriend or fiancé. Have I been mean or ignoring Javier?"

"No, but you have not really taken the time to talk to him. He is here almost every night across the courtyard from you and you still do not know much of anything about him," Susanna pointed out.

"So what are you suggesting?"

"Maybe dinner, a lunch by the pool, some beers, anything to show him you two have a connection beyond dealing with family drama."

Richard sighed, knowing his sister just wanted him to bond with her soon to be husband, "I will check with Mychal. We will let you know something."

"Great."

An idea suddenly struck Richard, "Can he pick wines for the annual gala? He is still a sommelier in training, right?"

Susanna smiled, "Yes and I will say yes for him."

"Good, tell him to drop by the house one night this week so we can work out the details."

The night of the annual gala Mychal was nervous and upset. Nothing fit and she was feeling guilty for leaving Carrigan. Richard found her sitting on the bed close to tears.

"What is wrong? Are you hurting?"

"No," a big fat tear escaped her left eye, "nothing fits right. What if something happens to the baby while we are gone? I think we should stay home or at least I should stay home."

"*Bella,* it has been over two months. We have only been to the doctor and back home. This is the first time that we moved the gala back to September and invited students and community leaders," Richard tried to sound understanding. "We have to go. I have to go."

"I know you are the chairman of the university board," she sighed.

He sat beside her and kissed her ear. "I am not concerned if your dresses are a little snug. Seeing your curves in a tight dress all night is a turn on just thinking about it."

He placed her hand in his lap to prove his point. Mychal felt a tremor as her

24

palm brushed against his semi-rigidness.

"I make you feel like that?" she teased, feelings of insecurity ebbing.

Richard kissed her neck, "Every time."

"Okay, I will go on one condition."

Puzzled, he asked, "Condition?"

"That you hold that thought until we get home."

"*Toda la noche mi amor*. Now we need to get this over with so we can get back."

The university gala this year was entirely too large to be held at the Garçia-Torrés home, so it was moved to a local hotel. Mychal managed to find a black strapless gown that she knew Richard would love the cleavage the dress created. From the moment they arrived people were talking, hugging, and pulling them in different directions.

An hour past their two-hour limit, Mychal was beyond ready to go home. As Richard engaged in another boring conversation with some super tall local government official she snuck away to the bathroom and called his cell phone. She told him to act like there was some urgent matter and meet her at the valet stand. Minutes after she arrived, he arrived with a wink, "Good plan."

"Actually, my breasts are starting to ache, so we need to go."

Once home she immediately fed the baby while Richard got the details of how Carrigan did her first time with Abeulita Carmen. He walked her to the cottage in the back of the property. He walked past the apartment noticing the downstairs lights were off. Tony must have been out and they left Susanna at the gala. Richard mentally patted himself on the back at his decision to move his siblings out and foster their independence.

Back upstairs Mychal was rocking Carrigan who was dressed for bed.

"Already had a bath?"

"Yes. She has been asleep since I fed her. I just wanted to hold her."

Richard smiled at his wife, "You are such a good mother. Who knew that beneath all that karate kicking, hard core professional was this soft mommy figure?"

"Oh shut up," she blushed.

"Oh wait, I knew," he teased, "and that is why I married you."

He walked over and kissed the baby good night. He whispered in Mychal's ear, "I need to shower. Care to join me? You know there is this spot on my back I can never reach."

"You are really feeling yourself tonight, aren't you?"

"I would feel better if your wet body was next to mine," Richard taunted.

"Just go," Mychal ordered him out, not wanting to show her excitement at his suggestion. Her husband was the perfect lover: unselfish, caring, permissive and sensuous.

After putting the baby down for the night, she eased into their room. Richard was in the shower and his naked outline on the other side of the glass ignited her desire. She joined him, taking the bodywash to soap his back. He let her bathe him wordlessly. She could not help notice how her actions were affecting him. Mychal made sure she paid attention to washing his thighs. Richard pulled her to him and kissed her passionately. His hand snaked between them so he could stroke her core. Mychal's breath caught at his movements. Her husband always knew what pleased her. She broke their kiss so she could taste his neck, nipples and anywhere else she desired.

"*Bella*, I need you now," was his strained command in response to her kisses. With both hands on her bottom, he lifted her up and onto him. Mychal locked her arms behind his neck and legs around his waist for support. Richard moved them against the wall for more support before getting down to the business of pleasing them both until the water began to run cool. After they exited the shower and dried off, Richard led Mychal to their bed where he again made love to his wife until they were exhausted.

Mychal stood in front of the mirror frowning. Richard was walking around burping the baby. He was also afraid to, but asked anyway, "What are you doing?"

"Wondering if I will ever get back into my party dresses."

"You looked great in that last dress for the annual gala," he rubbed Carrigan's back as she tried to hold her head up, blue-green eyes shining. "Look at daddy's girl. You want to see mommy and her new curves? I love her new curves, they look great. Say 'mommy do not worry'."

The baby hiccupped.

Mychal smiled at them but said, "I am not in shape."

"You did just have a baby a little over two months ago."

"I know, but I miss being physical, you know running and working out. At my six week checkup everything was fine."

Richard zipped out a comment with a hidden meaning, "I could have told you that."

"Honey, please be serious," she urged.

"I am," he played with Carrigan. "You could ask Abeulita Carmen to watch her so you can work out."

"I would but you will be worried that security cannot watch us both," Mychal reminded him.

Richard frowned. For once he had forgotten Demitri's accomplice or accomplices were still at large. "*Bella*, I am so sorry. I forgot we still need the security details."

Mychal heard the guilt in his voice, "Oh, please don't start. For a minute I forgot too. For a minute we had a normal life. Besides, I like Iroh, he has become my friend."

She walked over to him and kissed his cheek knowing that would not ease his guilt. "We will work something out. Quit worrying and definitely do not start feeling guilty. For the umpteenth time, it was not and is still not your fault."

Richard gave her a weak smile.

"I might buy a running stroller and Iroh could run with us."

"I can live with that," Richard was surprised by how her simple idea really eased his mind.

"When she gets older, then Iroh can train her in the arts. She can be a black belt by eight with multiple black belts by twelve," Mychal threw out, just wanting to see his reaction.

"*Como madre, como hija,*" he replied.

2

Intoxication and Maturation

It was decided that Iroh would work out with Mychal during the week. Overall Mychal's body was returning to its original shape. She silently patted herself on the back for her brilliant idea that appeased her husband and got Iroh to become her personal trainer slash martial arts instructor. She only studied one martial arts style, while Iroh studied five. So as the fall progressed, Mychal and Iroh developed a routine that consisted of running once a week and training two days a week. By Halloween, she lost most of the weight but the last seven pounds or so continued to linger.

The whole situation seemed to ease
Richard's mind as he planned to return
back to work full time after Thanksgiving.
Although Tony was handling the business
just fine, Richard felt his brother's attention
needed to be focused on finding Demitri's
accomplices. Only then would Richard
breathe a sigh of true relief. It would be the
only relief he would have as the rest of his
business was nearing train wreck status.
The company's finances were strained due
to extra security and business contracts on
hold until he could prove the company
troubles were resolved.

When Richard returned to work full-
time he intended to pour his efforts into
stabilizing the company's revenue while
improving relationships with existing
customers. He wanted to calm the fears of
current clientele, particularly his American
clients who were being difficult. More
importantly, Richard was pushing to
increase business with the start of the New

Year.

For Thanksgiving the whole family went to Richard's Uncle Rico's home. Mychal always thought his uncle was one of his parent's siblings, but found out this was one of his father's childhood friends who was like family. The day was fun but tiring. There was dancing, singing, wine, games and storytelling, especially by Uncle Rico who was a master orator with a rich baritone voice. It was late when she and Richard left, leaving Tony, Susanna and their significant others still dancing the night away. When they got home and settled the baby, Richard made slow passionate love to Mychal until the sun threatened to peak over the clouds. That was the first time Carrigan slept through the night.

During the holiday, Susanna approached Mychal about helping to plan her wedding. She was troubled when she spoke about her wedding plans. After a series of vague answers to Mychal's questions, she finally said, "Okay Susanna, what's wrong? What's really bothering you?"

Mychal's question hit home. Susanna broke down close to tears, telling the other woman she was not sure about having a large wedding. She told Mychal about Javier's mentality concerning pretentious, aristocratic people then swore her to secrecy. She finished by saying she wanted to consider Javier's feelings before anything else.

Mychal's response was, "That is . . . um . . . a lot of stuff you are dealing with."

Susanna sighed, "I know. I want something small, Richard says I need to incorporate the family and Javier just wants me happy."

"Can you keep it to less than two hundred people?"

"Of course I could, but there are people that were associated with my parents that my brother says I just must invite." She added, "He also said that since I am going into business for myself after graduation, I need to make connections now."

"Yeah, Richard mentioned your new company plans and I think it's a great idea. One that you will be your own boss and not working under your brothers in the family business, which I definitely picked up on," Mychal pointed out.

"You got it. And I get to incorporate my love of music. I have not started any planning. I will work on it after my wedding and during internship this coming summer."

Mychal winked, "Smart girl."

"Now we just have to get my wedding over and done."

It was decided the guest list would be kept to two hundred people or less. Mychal and Susanna would shop for dresses during and after the semester ended.

Mychal mentioned her plans with Susanna to Richard a few nights later. Though they were watching TV in bed, she heard the change in his voice when he said, "It is her wedding and I am just trying to help."

Mychal turned to him, "With that attitude what are you calling help?"

"What attitude?"

"That attitude you are showing right now. What's wrong now Richard?" she tried not to sound exasperated.

He sighed, "My sister is the only daughter of the notable shipping Garçia-Torrés family, a well-known name in this area. Though they are gone, my parents' name still means prominence, especially in business. I think that her wedding should not only be her day but also a chance to jumpstart her future business. Am I wrong for that?"

"No, but you are being a typical man." Then she paused as a thought dawned on her, "Wait one minute! Did you use our wedding as a business strategy of some kind?"

"Not exactly, I- "

Mychal cut him off, "Not exactly means that is exactly what happened. Richard, how could you?"

Richard put his arm around her to draw her close. When she resisted he said, "Come on Mychal, it is not like that?"

"Oh really? Then convince me it is something different by telling the truth."

"Yes, it really was different than what you think. I just invited a few business associates and family friends. Please do not be angry. I did not tell you because I truly wanted you to be excited about the day. I did not want you to worry about security, business partners or anything else other than enjoying your family," he hoped she understood.

"While your thoughtfulness was admirable, I question your increasing need to keep things from me. Just like the whole Demitri crashing my wedding thing. Dammit Richard, I'm supposed to be your partner in life, not some adult child who needs protecting from the things that you deem too much for me to handle," she pointed out.

Richard said nothing at first, then said, "It will not happen again."

Mychal responded, "I know it won't because we won't have another wedding, genius."

He gave her a sheepish look, "You know what I mean."

"Do I?"

"Come on *Bella*, let it go," he avoided

the topic. "Remember this is about Susanna, not us."

Mychal decided not to further fight about something she knew she was right about, but instead said, "Their wedding is about Susanna and Javier. He should have a say in his own wedding as well. Quit bullying them."

"I am not bullying them? You know that is excessive."

"Do you want to go into that behavior discussion tonight?" Mychal pulled completely away and crossed her arms, squared up ready for battle. "Because I am ready for that conversation on what is and is not excessive bullying."

His wife's posturing and her blazing eyes, let him know she meant business about having a conversation that he wanted and needed to avoid. Richard knew when he had lost. "Please not tonight or ever if possible. I feel like I am pushing them, but

in a loving way. Not in a bullying way.
And I will try not to keep things from you.
Husband's promise."

She huffed, "There is no such thing."

"It is now," he pulled her close for a
kiss.

Thanksgiving always signaled the
last two weeks of the semester. Susanna
was in the apartment studying when
Richard dropped by one night.

"*Hola* big brother. What do I owe
this visit?" she half joked.

He walked in and looked around,
"Where's Javier?"

"At his place."

"He has his own place. I am truly
shocked." Richard teased, "I thought he
lived here."

"Oh that is too funny. Did you come by to pick on me or did you come by for something else?" Susanna put her guard up.

"I came to talk about your wedding."

She rolled her eyes, "Here we go."

"Susanna, please. It is not like that," he tried.

"Then what is it?" she snapped back.

"I . . . I," Richard tried again, "I want you to have the best wedding possible. No pregnant brides, no security at the gate, nothing related to drama."

Susanna gave him a long look, "In other words, nothing like what you had at your wedding. But nothing that I, no we, want at ours."

"That is not what I meant. Whatever your heart desires is what I want for you."

"Are you sure you are being honest with yourself about that *hermano*? Every time we talk about this it seems like you are trying to steer me in the direction of a big event. *Cuanto más grandes, mejor.*" She paused then said in a less panicky voice, "We don't want a show. We are not up for Susanna and Javier the wedding production."

"Susanna, stop thinking of your wedding as a show. You of all people know the difference between a show and family events. Our family loves to celebrate and they want you, the only daughter of our parents, to have a memorable day. Can you blame them?"

"What about Javier? It *is* his day too," she replied quietly.

It finally dawned on him the real problem. Thinking carefully before he spoke, Richard said, "It just occurred to me that this whole situation might be intimidating to Javier. My marriage was under different circumstances, so I never really got to feel the excitement of a regular wedding day or the planning that goes in to it. *Hermana*, I am so sorry to be so insensitive."

She smiled at her older brother looking handsome and remorseful at the same time, "Ah, finally listening with your head and not your male ego. Now you got it."

"I will respect whatever you choose, but I cannot protect you from Uncle Rico, Uncle Juan, Uncle Alberto and Aunt Doris," Richard referred to his parents' various siblings and friends.

"I will talk to Javé at the end of the semester. I promise."

Richard hugged his sister, "Maybe I will take some time to get to know my future brother-in-law-beyond his excellent taste in wine."

"I would like that. He so wants to

impress you."

Puzzled he asked, "Why?"

"Because you are our patriarch and the person I still look up to like I did when I was a child."

His sister's confession made Richard blush.

With only a few words to his wife, Richard decided he was looking forward to knowing Javier beyond his relationship with Susanna. On one of his lunch breaks the following week, Richard dropped by Señor Plasençia's shop. When he walked into the shop, the smell of its age mixed with wine and some cheese was immediate. It reminded him of his grandmother's wine closet in the country.

Javier smiled uncertain but welcomed him, "Richard, what are you doing here? Is Susanna okay?

Taking a deep breath he replied, "Yes, she is. I came to see you."

"Me?"

"Yes, I thought I could get to know you a little better. You met my family in a time of turmoil which was both good and bad. Times like those bring out the best in people but also serve as a distraction to overlook things and people." Richard paused, searching for the right words to say next, "I was so busy in my own life that I never really got to know you beyond the person who reacts in a crisis. I wanted to go for a little lunch and learn who Javier is when he is not picking out wines and protecting my sister?"

To that Javier responded with a chuckle, "I am glad to know you are thinking of me beyond my jobs. I would like to say I could do that now, but Papa Plasençia is out and I cannot leave the shop."

Richard was not sure if he was being truthful, reluctant or both. So he said, "Well, how about we have a working lunch? Is there a place close by that you like? If so, call in something and I will pick it up. You can pick us out a wine to have with it."

Hesitantly Javier agreed, still unsure what to make of Richard's appearance with his olive branch bearing mission. He called in rice bowls from the shop two doors down. While Richard picked it up, Javier selected a pinot noir to go with their lunch that contained chicken with mushroom in an herb sauce. Lunch started out with Richard updating Javier in the lack of progress in the case at work. By the end of the first bottle they were talking about rugby. Into the second bottle they began to talk about Javier's future with Susanna and how their family intimidated him at first.

"I cannot apologize enough that I may have made you feel that way. It was unintentional. I guess I was so hyper focused on my wife and child that I was not myself," Richard felt a pang of guilt over another situation he created.

"I completely understand. I keep telling you that. Both your wife and Susanna have convinced me that you are a good guy who was under stress," Javier looked away. "I'm sure Susanna told you why I was basically uncomfortable at first."

"No, she has not and I respect that. Although we are family, your business is between you and her," Richard's brain was quite foggy from the wine. He could not figure out why Javier's attitude changed. "Plus, nothing she could tell me could persuade me that you are not the one for her. That is unless you are an axe murdering, serial killing alien from the moon."

"What?" the younger man looked at him like he was crazy.

"Sorry, been around my wife too

long. She speaks very colorful American to say the least," Richard blushed.

"Yes she does. I am glad you believe I am the one for your sister. I had a not so proper childhood and at one point I questioned whether I was right for her."

Richard gave him a bewildered look, "That is hard to believe. But go on, if you feel comfortable sharing, I want to hear this."

"My mother died when I was young and my important official father did not want his illegitimate love child by his mistress. So he sent me to an orphanage. Señor Plasençia, I mean Papa Plasençia, took me in and raised me as his own. Your sister suggested that I call him papa to honor him because he is my true father," Javier finished proudly.

"So, do you still love my sister?" Richard asked.

"Of course I do!"

"Then your background changes nothing. While Señor Plasençia is your family, we will be your family as well. But I need to know is this why you do not want a big wedding?" he had to ask.

"Yes. No. I mean I do not care one way or the other. I just want Susanna happy. She has told me that you want our wedding to be her introduction into the more corporate side of your business." Javier sighed, "She is caught between wanting to please you, her older brother and protecting me, her future husband."

At this Richard rocked back in his chair to think. Finally he said, "Like I told my sister, I will concede. She can have the wedding she wants. I will take people from my business that she has never met off the guest list. That way the wedding is smaller and you both are happy. *Sí*?"

"*Sí, gracias*," Javier seemed pleased.

The bell rang and Señor Plasençia

hobbled into the store. He looked at Richard and a wide grin spread on his face, "Señor Ricardo. *¿Qué es el placer. Cómo es Senna?"*

"*Senna es buena.* As always she sends warm wishes." Senna was Richard's aunt.

"Is she still good looking?" the old man laughed.

"Papa Plasençia!"

Richard laughed with the old man, "*Si*, she can still turn heads."

"Will she be at the wedding?"

"*Sí, bien como el infierno.*"

Both men laughed with Javier just shaking his head.

As he returned to his office the fog in Richard's brain was replaced by the beginning of a dull headache and the need for grease. When Tony came to his office, the blinds were closed against the afternoon sun and Richard was eating fries and a burger. His brother joked, "Did you close the blinds so your wife could not see you eating that? You know she says burgers are bad for your health."

"I know, but I needed some real food. That tiny healthy lunch I had with Javier was good but I think the wine sucked it up. My head is killing me."

His brother got a kick out of that, "Been hanging out with our soon to be brother-in-law. Nobody warned you he can really drink?"

Richard swallowed a bite of fries, "No and two bottles later, he is fine and I am dying at my desk by late afternoon."

"That's funny. Bet he was rock solid."

"Hell yes! I think I drank most of both damn bottles. I did find out he is a cool guy."

Tony smiled, "I could have told you that and saved you a headache."

"I would have believed you but still wanted to know for myself," Richard finished his second lunch.

"After you live with the guy for six months, you do have some idea what he is really like and whether he is right for your sister."

"True. What is on your mind?"

"I came to update you on the sabotage case. Between Evan and the police, they have obtained enough information to arrest Demitri's accomplice Iván Salamanca."

Richard became intrigued, "What happened?"

Tony replied, "Evan has been quietly passing around a picture of Salamanca and implying this person almost got everyone at the dock killed. One shift supervisor on the overnight remembered him. Said he was from some staffing service and worked long enough to be written up twice."

"What?"

"I know. Both write ups were about being in secured places without authorization. The first time was a warning. But get this; the second time was the night before the fork lift accident. He was recommended for termination and that is why he was never seen again," Tony finished with a triumphant smile.

"Where is he now?"

"Under surveillance. The authorities needed some help so Evan has some of the security personnel following him to make sure he does not disappear."

"Well done Tony! I knew you were the right person to get to the bottom of our company mystery," his brother's compliment made Tony blush.

"You know I want this over and done. If we get people to testify against Demitri, it will save the whole family a lot of unnecessary publicity and negative exposure. While we can handle it, the situation may not sit well with others."

Richard was a little confused, "Like who?"

"Loyal clients, potential investors, and my girlfriend."

Richard knew about the business part but was caught off guard by the last person Tony named, "What happened? I thought Yadira was different. If she stayed with you through the car accident, I thought she was a keeper for sure."

"She certainly could be, but she is not about any drama. She looked me up on the internet and saw some of my previous exploits with various girlfriends in the tabloids. She does not want to date someone with my reputation that might ruin her career."

For a second Richard stared at this new Tony sitting across from him. Until today he had not given much thought to how his brother's appearance had changed. Although he kept his gelled hair style, Tony wore a pinstriped shirt, solid tie, and tailored dark slacks. Richard noted before when Tony wore khakis and a company polo shirt that he was neat even down to his trimmed goatee. Occasionally, Tony would breeze into his office wearing a suit, but he assumed it was always for some meeting. His younger brother had morphed from extravagant playboy to astute business partner. Richard joked, "So Tony the old *canalla* still lurks around?"

"In a bad way; I wish I had listened to some of your advice. Now I feel I am behind the curve for my generation," Tony frowned. "I'm just now considering how a college education would help me in this business."

His older brother's face went slack with shock, causing him to laugh. Richard almost did not have words, "I . . . I do not know what to say. I mean wherever you are going with this or whatever you want to do, you have my support."

"Thanks *Hermano*."

Richard gave a half laugh, "The right woman made you want to do all this changing?"

Tony rose to leave, "Not just her, I guess this whole situation made me grow up fast. It also made me realize I have been taking much in life for granted. I saw how my efforts made a difference in keeping the family safe. I saw how I was selling myself short on being all that I could be. Then, two ladies changed my life. First, Yadira because she is uniquely normal, doing what real people my age should be doing with their lives. The second was Carrigan because she changed you, which let me know there is hope for me yet."

"Hey! I am not sure I know how to take that."

Tony chuckled walking toward the door, "Anyway you want, because it is true. *Roman, el viejo oso es ahora un padre.*"

Richard could not let that one pass, "*Y mi hermano ya no es canalla, sino que se ha convertido en un adulto.*"

"Whatever," was all he got back as the door closed.

3
Neighbors and Addicts

Christmas was great for the Garçia-Torrés family. Their morning was fun with the baby getting gifts that would eventually wear out their welcome due to their noise factor. Javier and Susanna exchanged gifts with them after breakfast. Javier gave her a double woodwind instrument called a dulzaina and she gave him an official soccer jersey. And a house key. Mychal could feel Richard's uneasiness as he sat on the floor with their daughter. He played it cool and helped the baby pull at the paper on her gift. After exchanging gifts, it was time to pack the car and go to Richard's

Aunt Edith's house. In the car ride he talked about everything but the house key until Mychal said, "Stop avoiding the elephant in the room. I saw that look on your face at the house key gift."

Richard laughed, "There was no look. You were just waiting for one and besides Tony told me about it last week."

"So you were ready for that little surprise?"

"Exactly."

Mychal gave him a dirty look, "At this point I appreciate you sparing me the whole 'Bella, Susanna gave Javier a house key' drama. However, I'm going to need you to stop cheating at life."

He just chuckled and drove on.

A little over two weeks after Christmas the semester started and Mychal was beyond pleased. She and Richard had some heated words behind her decision not to sit out the whole year. In the end, he conceded that her independence is what initially attracted him to her and to pressure her to stay home would change who she was. Her proposed schedule was what put his mind at ease about the time she would be away from home.

Mychal, who was very aware of their current situation, worked out some classes with Connie and Ruby. She would teach two classes on campus a couple of days a week, picked up a hybrid class and taught a completely online dissertation seminar course. Connie wanted the junior classical literature class in exchange for the graduate narrative and play writing course. Ruby was glad to take Mychal's sophomore composition class in exchange for ethics in journalism class. Mychal's half online, half in person hybrid course was research graduate writing, which went well with the dissertation seminar.

Tuesday and Thursday afternoons Richard would have to leave the office early to pick up the baby from Mychal's office. Iroh would stay until her classes were over then follow her home. Her hybrid class met six times during the semester and she and Richard would get Susanna or Abeulita Carmen to watch Carrigan. Before the semester started Mychal had collaborated the meeting dates with Richard before putting them in her syllabus online.

The night before her class Richard was restless. He tossed and turned until finally Mychal got up and switched on the light on his side of the bed to wake him up.

He sat straight up in a panic, "What's wrong?"

"I was about to ask you the same thing. You have been tossing all night long. I thought you were having a seizure or just a fight in your sleep. Richard, now confess if you ever want to sleep again, what is bothering you?"

He flopped back on the pillows,

"Nothing and everything."

Mychal kneeled beside the bed and gave him a straight look, "Are you worried about us again? Carrigan and I are fine."

"I know. I just believe that you are going back to work at a bad time. We are closing in on some people we think helped Demitri and I need to feel my family is safe until we actually catch them," he looked at the ceiling.

"Got it and again thanks for sharing," she noted sarcastically. Before he could interrupt she continued, "I already know you were trying to protect me from this information so don't even say that. I need you to trust the safeguards you have put in place for us. Also, I am not some weakling. I am probably lethal now than I was before our daughter. Richard, honey, give things a chance. If I go back to work and it is too much, then I will negotiate for an adjunct so I can take the rest of the semester off. Don't let your out of control anxiety derail this whole situation before it starts. Okay?"

He finally turned to look at her with red rimmed tired eyes, "I just want this whole mess to be over. I feel like I am in prison too."

Mychal's heart broke a little. She leaned in and kissed his forehead. "You have to change that attitude or Demitri and her terrible accomplices are winning the battle that was already declared a loss. Honey, you cannot control everything. Have a little faith that things will work out without you having to micromanage every little detail and contingency."

Richard made a face and rolled over. She turned out the light and got back in bed with him. She hugged her husband and gave him a solid good night kiss, "Get some rest. As the old saying goes, leave tomorrow to worry about itself."

She turned over and snuggled up

against his broad chest. Richard let out a long breath and pulled her closer, *"Gracias Bella*. I love you."

"I love you too. Now go to sleep. I have to go to work tomorrow."

As she settled in, Richard pulled her hips up against his evident desire. Mychal tried to ignore him by pretending she was already asleep. His hands caressed and manipulated her body until she gave in, knowing at the current rate she would never get any sleep that night.

It took Mychal a few weeks but she finally had a handle on being a working mother. There were a few bugs in the beginning with Richard picking up Carrigan, but the ever present Iroh was a tremendous help. By midterms in March, Mychal was confident she would be on track, schedule and all.

One Sunday night her brother Max

called. He was playful at first but Mychal got the feeling something else was going on. When she said so, he replied, "Yeah sis, we need to talk. Jacob's preliminary indictment hearing for new charges is in about three weeks. But the prosecutor wants to interview you."

"How? I can't come home with the baby and all. I just went back to work and Richard-"

"Okay calm down sis," Max interrupted her.

"Do you understand? I will *not* come home because I do *not* need this foolishness right now! I still can't believe his dumbass-"

"Mychal calm down!" he interrupted again, more forceful, "I told you this might happen. The prosecutor has reason to believe that you need to be interviewed as a possible witness in the case."

"What does that mean? Before I was

thought to be a partner and now I'm a witness?" Mychal was skeptical.

"It means that you would be interviewed via video conference. It would be recorded while Jacob's lawyer and the prosecutor ask various questions. You would have a lawyer present to keep you from answering any tricky questions that may lead to self-incrimination. So no, you do *not* have to come home and do *not* go bothering Richard about this conversation. I will call him and explain this new action on the case," Max insisted.

"Are you sure?"

"Yes sister. This whole thing will be easier than beating up a crazy ex-girlfriend then giving birth. Pun intended."

Mychal had to laugh at him, "Oh, you are too funny. But can we avoid or delay telling Richard?"

"No, because his Uncle Rico has to set up everything. Unless things changed since I spoke to him last week, that will still be your attorney, right?" Her brother sounded playfully doubtful.

"Well yes. Wait, you talked to Richard last week? He never mentioned that."

"We talk at least once a week which is why he probably didn't say anything." Then he teased, "What's wrong? Think someone else is stealing your husband's time? Don't be envious, it's not your style."

"You are beyond stupid Max, but love ya. Keep me posted on what to do next."

"I will. Kiss my niece for me. Tell the family I said hello. Love you too. Bye." Max hung up.

Richard was working hard on not keeping things from his family, especially his wife. But anything involving Demitri, he made an exception. He rang the bell at his neighbor's house and waited. The door was opened by a familiar face. Rafael's sister greeted him, "Richard, how are you?"

He hugged and kissed the older woman, "I am fine Felicia. How have you and the family been?"

"We are fine. Lucius is working on retirement. Our oldest Leto decided to become an ice barista in London and my girls Damariss and Dana are off to college in the next two years." She caught him up as they walked in the house. "I heard you had some stressful changes and congratulations are in order."

"Indeed. I love being married and my daughter is beautiful." He stopped and sighed, "Look, I cannot apologize enough for what has happened. I had no idea my ex would go this far. I wish-"

She cut him off, "Richard, nobody blames you. My brother has always picked *mujeres locas*. Unfortunately, this time this one went too far. It was literally almost the death of him."

"But I feel so bad," he tried again.

"At this point Rafael does not need pity. What he needs is to get some part of his life back. We both know that he will never be completely normal again, but I think your visit will help him." She ushered Richard into the living room and said, "The bones have healed but his spirit is still a work in progress."

Rafael's sister did not follow him into the room. Richard walked over to the panoramic window where his neighbor sat looking down. Rafael looked up from his reading. He reached for his cane but Richard stopped him, "No need to be so formal, it is just me."

The younger man smiled, "Good to see you old man. Though with this cane, I am sure that I look like the old man."

Richard sat in the chair adjacent to him, "Nonsense, it makes you look like a dashing movie character from a classic movie."

"You are full of *cagar*," Rafael laughed, "The way things have been going, it feels good to share a laugh with a friend. Can we share a drink too?"

"No thanks, the laugh will do. Believe me, I know there have been far too many tears."

"And bumps and bruises."

"Agreed," Richard concurred then said, "I am so sorry. I wish none of this happened."

The other man sighed, "You and me both. I wish I knew how things went wrong so quickly."

"I never knew she was so crazy. First she came after me, then you and finally Mychal."

"She came after you first," Rafael was surprised, "I had no idea."

Richard settled back in his chair, "When we broke up the first time she lied to the authorities and tried to have me arrested. When I decided that we could be civil, I thought she could handle me moving on. It began with little stuff after I got engaged. She vandalized my DB-7 until she totaled it."

"Eso sí que no!"

"Créanme es, tires, windshield then the body. I got rid of it and decided to drive the truck."

Rafael smiled again, "I remember when you got that car. I was so jealous. It gave you the appearance of intrigue, like some international spy. It was an instant magnet for women."

"Como sí. You were driving that Avendor, all sleek and black with the red rotors. I think it was the only one like it in

73

the city and everybody knew who you were. What happened to it?"

"I sold it and bought a red 599."

Richard was impressed, "Now, I am the jealous one. They are not build to hold kid's car seats "

Rafael looked back at the view and quietly said, "Guess I will not be driving that anytime soon or at all."

Neither man said anything for a minute. Richard broke the silence and asked, "Does Ferrari make a truck?"

That got a laugh out of his neighbor. "Now, there's an idea. I guess I should look into that considering my injuries. You know she really did a number on me. I still have no idea how I survived broken legs, three broken ribs and a concussion. The tip of one of my ribs was lodged in my stomach which caused a slow bleed. My saving grace was I kept my hiking supplies in the storage room in the back of the pool house. I had water and a few bags of trail mix. I was running low on water and hope when the authorities found me."

Richard was dumbfounded, "Nobody had any idea that you were missing? Not even your sisters and brothers?"

"She had them fooled. When they called she had an excuse for everything like I was gone, my cell phone was broken, or we were in the middle of doing something important. She had me fooled too. I thought we had something special despite the fact she still talked about you."

"What was she saying?"

"Things like how naïve you were and how much she hated Mychal. I just thought she was more bitter about the breakup than she wanted to admit. When I would question her about it she would just sex my doubts away," Rafael had a secret smile on his face.

"Been there, done that," Richard retorted dryly.

"The day I caught her looking at your house with binoculars was the day I could not deny it anymore. When I tried to kick her out, she beat me half to death with my own golf club. She dragged me into the pool house storage room and left me for dead."

"Again, I am so sorry," was all Richard could think to say. He had no words to express his current mixed emotions.

"It was not your fault. I did not blame you once I realized I only had myself to blame. I ignored the warning signs partially due to my own resentment. Even after the whole scene at the wedding I was stupid. I got her out of jail and we did not talk about it for days. Like I said, that day I caught her she reacted like a demon. The weird thing was when she came in with baby clothes. I was lying there in so much pain and she like cleaned up the bloody area with the clothes. That was weird.," Rafael conceded.

"She used them as a warning. Security found them before Mychal could." Richard frowned, "I am confused. What was your resentment over?"

"I hate to admit it, but I was jealous because of you. You got the most exciting person I had ever met and I wanted her. When I met Mychal she had such a bold and beautiful attitude. You seemed so uninterested in her that I thought I had a chance to get with her. That was until the night of the university gala when she flipped me over her shoulder. The next day you came to tell me to back off your houseguest. I was the one totally confused. At first you gave the impression that you were not even attracted to her, then you came off as if you were claiming her as a future conquest."

"Did I?" Richard joked, "I do not

remember saying she was a future conquest."

"You did not use those exact words but I got the underlying message that you were more than friendly with her. For you to actually come by the house on a Tuesday afternoon to make small talk about the party and family, I knew it was about something else. You made sure before you left that I understood she was off limits to me and everybody else."

"If it makes you feel any better, she attacked me too that night."

Rafael replied, "Wow, she was really drunk and hot-headed."

Both men sat in an uncomfortable silence. Richard broke it by saying, "I do not know if you heard but Mychal hurt Demitri really bad in the attack. Broken bones and everything. If it had not been for Tony, it is questionable what would have happened. He said when he arrived home that Mychal was enraged."

His neighbor was shocked, "No, all I knew was she was in jail awaiting trial."

"First she tried to run Mychal off the road but did not know it was actually my brother in my wife's car. He walked away banged up pretty bad. When that failed, she came to the estate and stabbed two of the security guards before attacking my wife." Then Richard said with pride, "But she was ready for her. Though Demitri injured the dog, Mychal broke her wrist and shattered her knee. Again, I think it might have been worse but Tony intervened."

Rafael's facial expression was a mix of emotions which went from grim to astonishment. Finally he said, "Damn! Your wife is intimidating to say the least."

"I know. If she was not pregnant, she would have really done some damage and this would be a different conversation altogether."

"I bet."

Richard rose to leave, motioning for Rafael to stay seated, "I know Mychal got the better end of the situation. But like I said before, we all have scars from this circumstance, some external and some internal. I just hope someday we will all move on."

Rafael nodded, "Time will tell."

"True. I hope this trial will go quickly. I want everyone to start the healing process."

"Maybe she will agree to a plea deal and we can all avoid more unpleasantness." Then, he said bitterly, "Or maybe she will get killed in a prison riot and there will be no need for a trial. It would be justice if she never made it to a trial at all."

Slightly uncomfortable at the other man's comments, Richard stood beside

Rafael to put his hand on the other man's shoulder for reassurance. "Do not let yourself get worked up over her. You just concentrate on getting better and getting back into that car. I really do not think Ferrari makes a truck."

That lightened the other man's mood and he laughed, "I will and thanks for the visit."

"Anytime. I am here if you need me," Richard offered before leaving.

The office was quiet and the tension thick with anticipation. Richard paced the floor, Tony checked his cell phone and Evan was at the computer, all waiting for any communication from the authorities at any moment. Evan received a text earlier from his security team that they were to cease all surveillance and clear the area as the authorities were going to raid the house. Richard went to his office bar and poured a drink.

Tony looked up and said, "Are you actually drinking before lunch? You need to keep your head in the game today. We might have to go to the police station in a little while."

Richard gave his brother a dirty look as he downed his scotch in one gulp then followed it with soda. "That was for last night when I paid Rafael a visit. Seeing him like that was drink worthy. Today I am fine."

"Liar," Evan shot over from the computer. He looked up and said, "Trust me, I empathize with your feelings. We all want this nightmare to end, but I still agree with Tony. No more drinks."

Silence fell back on the room again. Richard sat at his desk to review new marketing packages when the desk phone rang piercing the quiet as if it were a fire alarm in a school hallway. He snatched the phone up and barked a greeting. "Wait, let me put this on speaker."

"Señor Garçia-Torrés we placed surveillance on the house for twenty four hours while we obtained the warrant. An hour ago officers entered the premises. The place was chaotic and disheveled. The furniture was destroyed and every drawer in the house was emptied, leaving papers scattered everywhere. We found Señor Salamanca in his garage, dead in his car with a needle in his arm."

The group at the desk was so muted the detective said, "Are you still there señors?"

Richard cleared his unexpectedly dry throat to regain his voice, "We are Detective Pharr. Just at a loss for words."

"I understand. The whole scene put me and my partner at a loss for words as well. The house was in pieces and reeked of gas. There were holes in the walls, mattresses were cut open and all manner of food was out of the cabinets and covered the floor. Chairs and pillows were ripped apart and clothes were scattered all over the place. Whatever money or valuables someone was looking for, it is questionable whether they found anything. Either that or somebody broke in looking for drugs."

Evan looked at his crowd skeptically but said toward the phone, "How did this happen? You did say you had the house under surveillance, right?"

Detective Baird's voice came back over the phone, "It that Señor Barbosa? Your little group of paramilitary men were interfering with an investigation so I sent your pretend black ops boys home."

"Maybe if you kept them in place, Señor Salamanca might still be alive. Again I question how something like this happened under the keen watch of Madrid's finest."

"Wait you did say a burglar or drug addict?" Tony interrupted, "You think a burglar killed him with an overdose?"

Detective Pharr answered, "We are not sure what to think. We have no idea when it happened. Once the corner gives us a time of death, we can narrow down the time frame. We cannot say for sure whether it was suicide or homicide. People who confront an intruder are normally not found dead in a car from an overdose. It could have been someone he knew. The crime scene was a strange one that will take days to figure out. I am sorry Señor Garçia-Torrés. I wish I had more answers.

Richard spoke up, "You have told me what you can and for that I, no we, thank you. Keep me informed if there is any way I or my people can help."

"Will do," the detective hung up. The three men looked at the phone.

Tony asked, "Evan, what did you make of that interesting information?"

"I think the man's house was

destroyed looking for drugs or something like the detectives said. In this circumstance, nothing can be taken for granted."

"Why?"

"Richard, burglars snatch easy things like jewelry and computers. They get in quick and leave to avoid the job becoming messy. Addicts looking for drugs are not cutting open mattresses and pillows. They are looking in the backs of freezers, toilet tanks and ceiling panels where addicts usually hide their stash. Then they might take a computer or television to sell. Something about what the detective said does not add up. If Salamanca walked in on a person stealing his stuff, there would have been a fight or struggle. If he invited someone in the house that turned on him, there would have been indicators that he defended himself. How did a ransacked house end up with the owner overdosing in his car in the garage of that same house?" Evan posed the question.

Richard looked grim, "Something about this bothers you?"

"I am bothered because the crime scene does not match the behavior of the person meticulous enough to have pulled off the shipping and dock incidents. Does it seem logical that Salamanca was detailed enough to hide sabotage but not so careful in hiding his own drug stash? Does it make sense that he let someone in just to help him look for his own drugs just to overdose? I bet upon further investigation more inconsistencies will be found almost as if the mess left was to cover the true crime," Evan sounded bitter. "I also doubt a true addict would overdose in his car in his own garage. Why not use in his own house, steps away?

Tony inquired, "I'm slow here Evan. Come clean and tell us what's wrong?"

The security chief noisily exhaled,

"Gentlemen, I thought we had one psychopath and her accomplices to deal with. Now, we have a new player in the mix, possibly a professional killer, which has added another level of threat to the situation."

Richard suddenly felt sick at the weight of protecting his family dropping from his shoulders to the pit of his stomach.

4
Snooping and Teething

"*Hermana* I was considering moving out but I don't think that is possible in the immediate future. I am changing my plans to work it in my long-term goals," Tony told his sister as they walked to the house from the apartment.

"Why would you want to move out? We just got the apartment together. Is it Javier? I can tell him to go home more."

"No, I have been thinking you and Javier could have this place and maybe I could get my own. Later, Yadira and I could move in together."

Susanna stopped walking, "Wait; slow down. Didn't you tell me that you wanted to take classes to earn your degree and that Richard is adding more security?"

"I did."

"Then why do you think it would be a good time to move out at all? Is that girl pressuring you because I will talk to her and Mychal will enforce what I say if that is what needs to happen?"

Tony held up his hands, "Whoa! I need you and Mychal, who doesn't know what you are trying to volunteer her for, to chill. Yadira is not pushing me, I am pushing myself to-"

"That is so evident," his sister shot back.

"I am pushing myself to improve overall," Tony finished. "I want to earn my degree for me and want to move out so I can really show Yadira I am not the old Tony and totally committed to taking us to another level."

"Oh I'm sure you already know her on another level," Susanna rolled her eyes.

"Just stop. What is wrong with you anyway? You have Javier and Richard has Mychal. Why can't you just be happy for me?" Tony could not believe his sister's attitude.

"Because I don't want to gain a fiancé and lose a brother," Susanna looked away.

Tony let her words sink in, "*Hermana*, you will always have me. We are twins remember? I had your back even before we were born. I shared mom's shrimp diablo with you in the wound."

"You are so dumb."

"We will always be a close family because that is how mama and papa raised us. I know this new twist in the stuff going on at work is bothering you because it bothers all of us. But trust me, you will not lose me. I have been thinking about life a lot and was just sharing my thoughts of moving out in the not so distant future."

"It's great to see you actually thinking of the future," she replied. "It's just a scary time right now. Please stay Tony. At least until everything is resolved."

Tony could see Susanna was really disturbed by his news about finding the accomplice dead but did not show it at the time. She had obviously been thinking about it more than she let on. Finally he said, "I promise to stay until this mess is over.'

"Dar gracias hermano."

"For my sister, anything," he kissed the top of her head, "come on, let's go play with Carri."

Mychal waited until the right time to talk with Richard about her concerns. They had just finished a mock interview with Uncle Rico and were driving home to get Carrigan from Susanna.

"Honey, I need to say something."

"I'm all ears," he replied, giving her his attention while never looking away from the road.

"This whole thing with Jake could get muddled and I want to keep it from affecting your company and your reputation. I'm worried if people know about my situation through any American news outlets, you could be affected."

Richard chuckled, "You mean make it worse than now?"

"Have these incidents really effected your reputation to the point that it hurt the business?" she was curious but almost afraid to hear the answer.

"Yes and no. The company was built when I was a toddler, so it has over a thirty-year national presence. Until recently, I never had any problems so when things got crazy, many of my usual clientele understood. A few recently acquired accounts decreased the business by not offering me any new contracts. Keep in mind I still had their old contracts, meaning I did not really lose their business. The big celebration we had for the fourth was also a chance to win back the confidence of some of my uncertain clients. It was a celebration, but also a networking party. I knew you were being a great hostess so I took the opening to win over my doubting consumers."

Mychal had to admit she was impressed. Richard was always so giving and patient with her. She had no idea what a cunning business professional he was. She said, "Here I thought we were just celebrating the fact that I didn't kill

Demitri."

He smiled, "We were doing that and a few other things. The party was a costly and extravagant affair, but in business it is an investment in prospective gains. For the first time ever the company was in a single digit profit margin."

"Do I need to pick up some extra thesis classes? Or write another book?" Even though she knew they probably did not need the money, Mychal wanted him to know she would be willing to do whatever was necessary to help ease his stress.

"Really Mychal? I am trying to keep you at home with little success." He gave her a secret smile, "But I have considered hiring a private entertainer. You know someone who might give me a lap dance every so often."

"You want a lap dance?" she flirted, "Are you taking applications? Can I apply in person?"

"Stop, I need to pay attention to the road," he warned.

"You started it. I think I have something black to audition in," Mychal teased.

"You are going to see what kind of application process I have in mind when we get home."

"That's what you think. Your daughter might have other plans."

Richard gave her a wicked smile, "My plans are to work on her brother."

"You are a cunning dirty old man."

"Yes and one that cannot wait to get home."

"Richard, do you really want another baby in the middle of this unfinished business?" Mychal hoped she did not sound rude, just insecure.

"Since I did not get twins the first

time, I want our kids to be close in age. That way we can get them all out of the house at the same time," he reasoned.

"You wanted twins?"

"Yes and no. *Bella*, every man secretly wants twins. It shows his *ego masculino* or male prowess." Richard gave her a wink, "But if we did not get them the first time, I was looking forward to trying again."

"For a second time, you're a dirty old man."

"As long as you will have me."

Mychal changed subjects back to their previous topic, "So what does it mean if the company only made a single digit profit margin?"

He sighed, "It is all very complicated. The minor shareholders are family members but still expected a return on their investment. After charitable donations and creating a company position for Tony, the profits were skinny to say the least. So I passed it down to the workers because the human resource contractor already got paid a percentage per employee. Security and insurances were increased and factored into the company's profit margin."

Mychal was touched. She looked at him in awe, eyes moist.

Richard looked at her then back to the road, "What?"

"That was thoughtful."

"I guess," he lightheartedly replied, "the truth is, it happens to be a good business practice. The workers were in danger because of me. I had to show them in some way that I appreciated their commitment in these difficult times. It is nothing compared to what their lives are worth. They felt compensated. I keep good workers, which cuts cost of hiring new people. Everybody is happy."

After pulling into the garage and killing the engine, Mychal put her hand on his to get his attention. She quietly asked, "And what about you? Are you happy?"

He turned to face her, pulling her hand to his mouth to kiss it, "I am beyond happy. This is the life I was made for."

Mychal let a tear slip down her cheek, "I love you."

"I will always love you. Now I will get our daughter and you can start dinner. The sooner we get through dinner and put her to bed we can get down to unfinished business. Somebody owes me a job interview."

Richard had been to one crime scene too many in the last year. First the dock, then his home and now this abysmal place someone once call a home. The detectives asked him to come to Iván Salamanca's house roughly a week after it was processed as a crime scene. Nothing had been moved. Just as the detective said previously it was a mess. The cut open pillows and cushions were still askew in the living area, books and papers were scattered around everywhere and furniture was overturned. The gas smell was not as strong as the detective said but the scent still lingered. He peeked in the kitchen to see that too was in disarray. Canned goods littered the floor, along with pots and pans. His security chief made a face.

"What was that for?"

Instead of answering, he asked the detective, "Now what did you say happened here?"

Detective Baird replied, "Our best guess is some kind of drug frenzy. When we found Salamanca, he had empty vials in the back seat and a burnt spoon on the dash. The needle was still in his arm."

"Right," Evan moved around the room, testing certain parts of the floor. "Was the garage destroyed as bad as the rest of the house?"

"No Evan, I mean Señor Barbosa. What are you doing if I may ask?"

"Checking for creaking boards." Then he scanned the walls before stopping at the desk, "Computer?"

"Forensics did not discover one."

He moved the desk and more papers fell on the floor, "There was one here and a wireless router too."

Richard asked, "How do you know?"

"The cable line to the router has been cut. Always quicker than unscrewing it. The wire was covered by the desk."

The desk struck Richard as odd so he pushed more junk off to clear the top to see it his suspicions were right.

"Señor I know this is a messy crime scene, but I'm asking you to please not make it worse," the detective was regretting bringing them to the dead man's house already.

"This is a Harold Nollé desk."

"A what?" Evan asked.

"A Harold Nollé original. I inherited my mother's when she passed. The real question is what is a drug addict doing with a ten-thousand-dollar antique desk?" Before either person could answer, Richard opened the top drawer on the right and the bottom drawer on the left.

"Again Señor Garçia-Torrés, please do not alter the crime scene just in case we have to come through to take additional photos. As a matter of fact-"

Richard interrupted her, "You got a glove or something?"

She huffed but complied by fishing a glove out of her pocket and handing it to him.

"These desks have secret compartments, like so," he pulled out the smaller drawer on the right and dumped its contents on the desk. He laid the empty drawer upside down on top of the clutter. Next, he pushed down in the middle then slid a rectangular panel back to reveal a hidden compartment.

"Wow," was all Evan could say.

"Detective, I think you need to take these items in as evidence," Richard showed them the hidden compartment's visible contents: a stack of IDs, a few passports and a cell phone.

"I need my evidence bag," she turned to leave.

"Wait," Richard stopped her, "there are other drawers to open."

He pulled out the larger drawer on the left and sat it beside the other one. Evan and Detective Baird moved in to see what he was doing. "There is a small lever in the back. You push it in and up and the side panel releases."

Richard did as he explained and the side panel flopped open to reveal a bulging manila envelope and two shell casings.

"Okay, I need to call the forensic team back now," Detective Baird stepped out to make her call, "Do not touch anything else. I mean it."

"Yeah right," Evan began to look around other parts of the house as soon as she left.

Richard too ignored her warning. He walked past the bathroom to the only bedroom. It too was in shambles. It looked like the entire contents of the dresser were emptied in a pile and the cut open mattress was propped up against a chair. The closet's contents were scattered everywhere. He walked over to the window to see if the detective was still outside. Being in a dead man's house and finding his secrets gave Richard the creeps. He pulled back the curtain, though gentle, and the whole rod came off the brackets. He was quick enough to catch it before it hit him, but not before something falling out of the decorative knob end fell on his face before hitting the ground.

"Señor Garçia-Torrés are you okay?" He heard Detective Baird coming down the short hall. Quickly, he moved his foot to cover the black object with the toe box of his shoe. "I am fine. I just forgot this place is still an unstable mess."

She appeared in the doorway.

Richard smiled nervously holding the curtain rod, "It fell."

"Well put it back up and come on. Forensics is on its way and I do not want them to know you were in any other rooms after the evidence was found. Where is your intrusive security man?"

"Checking the garage I think." When she moved on Richard put the curtain rod back and what fell, a black micro USB card, in his pocket. Whatever was in the desk the police could have but for some reason this item was hidden differently and he wanted to know why.

"What are you doing?" Richard asked Mychal as she sat on the floor with Carrigan and a baby mirror.

"Teaching our baby to crawl, Ruby told me to try this trick." She held the mirror so the baby could see her own reflection. She let the baby touch the mirror then put it slightly out of her reach. At first the baby frowned up to cry. Mychal put the mirror closer and encouraged her daughter to crawl to get the other baby in the mirror. Carrigan looked at her mother as if to say 'what is wrong with you woman?'

Seeing Mychal and the baby on the floor, Solomon came to investigate. He had been gentle with Carrigan from the day she was brought home. He licked her arm and she giggled. Mychal pulled out his squeaky toy so he would leave them alone. He sat by Richard's chair chewing the ball to make it squeak. Mychal encouraged Carrigan to crawl to her but the dog suddenly had the baby's interest. She ignored her mother and half crawled to the dog.

"Richard, get your phone and video this. I want my mom to see this."

"What?" he looked up from his laptop.

"Look at the baby."

He looked at Carrigan trying to get to the dog and smiled. Richard took the ball to throw it. "Mychal, move closer to the fireplace and call him."

She caught the ball and moved, "Come on Solomon. Come get it."

The dog went to get his ball with the baby watching. No sooner than he laid down and began to chew, the baby was trying to move in his direction.

"Wait, let Papa help you," Richard sat her up on all fours so she could crawl. Carrigan moved timidly at first, then made a beeline for Solomon and his squeaky toy, half crawling and half dragging her legs. Richard smiled at Mychal who grinned back.

"We are in for it now," she warned.

"Yes we are."

Richard's prediction was accurate. Soon after Carrigan started crawling, she began teething. She was beyond cranky and fussy, driving her parents to the edge of fatigue. Mychal and Richard took turns getting up with the baby. A week after her seventh month birthday, the baby's first two teeth poked through her bottom gums and she began sleeping a little longer at night. While adjusting through the teething phase, Richard met Evan at the house to discuss his find at the crime scene. He waited until the afternoon because he knew Evan swam a few mornings during the week if the weather permitted. He showed up in chinos, polo shirt, sandals and his signature ponytail. The only thing his security chief said was, "You don't trust our detective friends?"

"Of course I do," Richard replied, "but I think it is time to take our little in house investigation to another level."

"It took you long enough," Evan huffed.

"I think we may need the kind of investigation the police are too . . . um . . . ethically bound to conduct."

"Oh, I thought that after the forklift incident. But I know you, being the upstanding business man, would not dare go that route."

"That was then, this is now. Evan, I have a better understanding of what the role of the authorities are in this situation," Richard looked at his daughter sleeping in her swing. "Their job is to catch the criminals and in the process ensure the safety of people. However, it is my job to protect my family and the people who pledged loyalty to my company."

Evan gave his boss an unimpressed and skeptical look, "Ideas?"

"I need one or two people with a special skill set, one that may require a grey area of what is lawful."

"Go on," Evan leaned in; his grey eyes were suddenly bright with anticipation.

"I need a person who can navigate

behind the public eye. Behind the normal access of information most regular people have." His security chief said nothing so he continued, "I need things done by a ghost."

Evan gave the other man a quirky look and smiled, "You need a hacker don't you? What are you thinking?"

"Depends on what is on that drive. If there are many financial records, the plan is to follow the money trail. But like I said, I need to make sure this is done invisibly," Richard emphasized the last word. "Until we get a better picture of everything and everybody at play here, I think stealth is needed to keep our actions from being revealed too early. After we know everything, then I might need a different kind of ghost."

"If this is going where I think, I don't like it boss man. We have already seen what happens to people when dealing with that type of professional."

"That is not what I mean. What I need is more brain than muscle. We will know exactly what we will need after the first ghost does his or her job."

Evan shook his head in agreement, "I got you. Give me a few weeks and I will have someone. Whoever is behind all of the attacks will not see us coming until it is too late."

5

Testimonies and Transactions

"Now Mrs. Garçia-Torrés, am I to understand that you did not know anything about where the money your brother-in-law, Jacob Adams, was investing came from?"

Mychal sighed and began again, "I have stated previously that he told me-"

Uncle Rico interrupted her, "Mr. Anthony, my client has answered that question seventeen times according to my count. Do you have another question or are you just trying to see if she has a different answer each time?"

On the video link the prosecutor turned to the judge, "Your honor, there is a line of questioning here, if you will give me a little leeway."

"All you get is a little, so make your point quickly. I too am tired of that same question as well," the judge replied dryly.

Uncle Rico motioned for her to answer the question. "Jacob told me he got grants from the government for a small business startup company."

"So you did not help him search for the applications, pick certain grants to apply for or even assist him with filling out the applications with your information? Anything?"

"No, I was an investor who was making up the difference of what the company needed for startup funds."

"Why did he put your name on the application?"

"I did not know he put my name on any application until you told me today," Mychal was trying not to show her frustrations at learning the information less than an hour earlier.

Uncle Rico spoke up as soon as she finished her statement. "Mr. Anthony, I know I have stated this for the record previously, but could you clarify again how my client's information was used on the application? When you make blanket statements without specifics, it leads to a misunderstanding or misleading information in the court records."

The assistant district attorney sighed heavily but replied, "The then Dr. Ayscue was on the applications as a reference."

"Thank you sir. Your honor, please let the record show again that my client was on the application as a reference only."

The judge rubbed her temples, "Noted. Move on Mr. Anthony"

"Where did you get the investment money from? Did you personally receive any grants?" Then Mr. Anthony added, "Did you receive any federal grants for your necessary contribution to help with the company?"

Mychal was insulted, "No, I did not receive any grants, government or otherwise. My funds came from the royalties from my book sales."

"But eventually you knew about the grants and how he misused the money. At what point was that a factor in whether you stayed in business with Mr. Adams?"

"No sir, I-"

"So why did you pull out of the quote unquote startup venture and risk losing your own personal money?"

"Your honor," Uncle Rico cut in, sounding edgy and perturbed.

"He is right Mr. Anthony. I gave

you a chance," the Honorable Judge Hardy-Heppard seemed bored.

Mr. Anthony kept going as if neither the judge nor her attorney spoke. "So why did you pull out of the business?"

Mychal felt her temper rise. This whole process felt more like she was on trial, not just being questioned about her involvement. Though Uncle Rico warned her it would be this way, he did not tell her that the prosecutor was going to be so rude. She had half a mind not to answer out of spite. Instead she took the passive route and said, "As I have said before, I did not help write the grants because I did not know anything in particular about the grants other than he said he obtained them through a government start up program."

"So what did you know about his side of the investment?"

"All I know about his side of the investment was he said he got government grants. He said specifically start up grants and I did not ask anything further." She paused, choosing her words carefully, "And as far as why I pulled out of the business, I noticed the things that Jacob proposed in the business plan were not being followed. I saw no additional investors. The new building plans never got the funding as he said. Nothing was progressing despite the revenue increase. The profit margin grew more every year, but the overall business growth was almost non-existent. After asking to look at the books for months, I finally got my wish. The ledger he gave me was so messy and disorganized that I could not make sense of anything. The fact he gave me a paper leger and not access to a computer printout or program was disturbing. I am not a business mogul, but I knew enough to know if the financial account files were antiquated and messy then my money was being handled messily as well. I wanted out after that."

"So you saw proof of the grants? Where is that ledger now?" he pressed.

"I did not say I saw proof of anything. Like I said, the ledger was a wreck. Sir, seeing that ledger was almost four years ago, so I have no idea where it is now."

"But you are saying there are records that exist and you have a copy of them?" The district attorney was attempting to open a new line of questioning.

"Sir, I do not have a copy of anything. I gave that joke of a record keeping attempt back to my brother-in-law when I demanded to get out of the business. I think you have a copy of my letter dissolving my interest in the company, correct?"

"Your honor if I may, I have a few questions for Mr. Anthony." Mychal was surprised when Richard's uncle spoke up. She wondered what he had up his sleeve.

"I am sure he will not mind as we have been so gracious to answer all of his on, off script, and multiple questions."

The judge pondered a moment before agreeing with words of precaution.

"Mr. Anthony, have you established a proper time line for when the grants were received, when my client initially invested, when both of the monies were misused and when my client pulled out based on her dissolving her association with her brother-in-law, Mr. Adams?"

"Well yes," the prosecutor answered slowly, wondering where the question was leading.

"Were your line of questions to ensure her testimony confirmed that fact?"

"Yes."

"Confirm or confuse?" her lawyer's accent seemed heavier the more his sweet old lawyer façade wore off. It was replaced by the pure professional that Mychal was glad she was related to. Though he gave the appearance of a pleasant white haired retired city bus driver in a tailored suit, she knew by his shift in stature, that he was all business. His tone reflected a new sternness, "Your line of questioning has been very suspect Mr. Anthony. You have badgered my client with multiple rewordings of the same question as if you are trying to catch her in a lie. You have been treating my client the same as a hostile witness, except you have not gotten permission from the judge to do so. You, Mr. Anthony, have been so disrespectful that you have not even addressed my client by her proper title the entire day. Moving forward you will address my client by her proper title which is Dr. Garçia-Torrés. To do otherwise is a cultural insult. Now while I am sure you are just trying to do your job, it has been done poorly, unprofessionally and borderline unethically."

The prosecutor was flabbergasted, "Unprofessional and unethical? Your accusations are absurd. I have never been culturally- "

Uncle Rico did not let the man finish, "My office will have a motion to suppress my client's testimony on your desk within the next twelve hours. Since you said you did your homework, you will not need this witness' testimony for your case. Your honor with all due respect, I feel that this action is in order due to the prosecutor's behavior."

Mr. Anthony turned to the judge, "Your honor!"

The judge sighed heavily and wiped her glasses, "Gentlemen, gentlemen, please put our egos away. Hold on Señor Nuaze-Piedra, do not send anything just yet. We are going to break for lunch with an extra thirty minutes so I can deliberate over the current behavior in my court room this morning. Court is in recess."

The judge banged the gavel to signal recess and the bailiff instructed everyone to rise. Moments later Mychal's video feed was cut off and she finally breathed a sigh of relief. When she turned to Richard's uncle he was all smiles, back to the good natured Uncle Rico who always reminded Mychal of the barrel chested owner of the Ponderosa Ranch, Ben Cartwright, from the Saturday afternoon western television shows.

"Are you okay my dear?"

"I'm just tired. I'm not sure what happened. What did you say Uncle Rico?"

He chuckled, "I called him on his behavior. The repetitive questions are a form of badgering a hostile witness. He has to ask permission from the judge to treat you as such. If he had taken that route, I would have objected. She knows he was trying to be slick. The fact I was ready to file a motion to have your entire testimony stricken from the record would affect his case. The fact I would have had it overnighted indicated I meant business. Without your testimony, his case will lose its legs. I will not be surprised with what she says after lunch."

Mychal was relieved, "Oh I get it."

"We have an hour my dear, so contact Richard to see if he can meet us for a late lunch. I would love to see my great niece."

Richard was able to meet them for lunch with the baby. Seeing Carrigan made Mychal feel better. Her daughter was a little cranky from teething. After Mychal fed her and made sure she burped, she massaged the baby's gums which seemed to sooth her.

The two men were engaging in deep conversation in both English and Castilian Spanish. Mychal could make out Uncle Rico was telling Richard about the proceeding. He promised that the badgering would stop and that his office had already prepared a motion to disregard Mychal's testimony based upon the biasedness of the prosecutor. At that, Richard's body language conveyed he relaxed a little. He rubbed her shoulder and said, "I knew Uncle Rico had this situation well under control."

Next, the two men launched into a business conversation about changes to some local policy. Mychal took the chance to change the baby. When she came back it was time to go back to court. When Carrigan went to her dad she immediately cried. Even with Richard consoling her she would not quiet down. It was agreed she would stay with her mother, who hoped they would be finished with the questioning within the next hour. A quick swap of keys versus car seats and Richard was on his way to the office.

On the short ride back to the lawyer's office, Carrigan dozed off, making her mother feel better. While the video link was reestablished, she left the baby in her carrier to sleep, beside Uncle Rico's desk.

By the time they linked in, court was just starting back in session and the judge was talking about the difficulties of the case. She acknowledged the two on video link but continued with her speech. She recognized that while Mychal testified to the facts that she was aware there were government grants, there was no proof that she was the recipient nor benefited from these grants. All Mychal's testimony proved was that her knowledge of the grants did not indicate her understanding of the true nature of what the money was used for at the time. Her testimony did however prove that Mr. Adams had a record keeping system. If the prosecutor could produce that system, then it needed to be decided whether to introduce it as new evidence.

The judge thanked Señor Ricardo Nuaze-Piedra for his time and patience with the court. In addition, she apologized to Mychal for any uncomfortable feelings and thanked her for her time before releasing her for the day. The judge reminded Mychal that she could be called back at a later date if needed. When she was done, Uncle Rico offered a few words of gratitude and comments about the judge's wisdom, which made her blush. After parting niceties of 'no hard feelings' to the defense attorney and prosecutor, he terminated the link. Mychal slumped back in her chair.

"Glad that is over?" he asked.

"God yes! I am so tired Uncle Rico."

"I am sure you have been through a lot."

Mychal closed her eyes to hold back her tears. She needed a moment to compose herself. She felt big male hands put a tissue in hers and squeeze it. Grateful for the support, Mychal wiped her eyes. She looked up and saw the older gentleman smiling kindly at her.

He sat next to her and said, "My dear everything is okay. You and my godson have been through more in one year than some people deal with in a lifetime. Throughout the whole thing, you have depended on each other for support. And when you needed more support than each other had to give, that is when you had the support of this family."

Mychal leaned over and hugged him, "Thank you Uncle Rico. I needed that."

"I know. Believe me, I know. I see you trying to be everything for Richard, be a new mother and hold down a career. He is doing the same thing, keeping the company afloat, being a new husband and a father that protects his family."

"At least that mess is over. That crazy bitch is in jail."

"To stay," Uncle Rico added. "I

remember when Richard called me to ask for help with her, the business and you. He was so overwhelmed but acknowledged the one bright spot in all the chaos was you and his unborn child. He was so animated when he talked about you that I knew he finally found his soul mate."

Mychal blushed.

"I was glad to hear it. Richard has always had a soft spot beneath that hard exterior he developed. He was a loving child but was a bit of an old soul. He both loved and admired his parents so much that he dedicated his life to making them proud. Honor society, swim team, soccer, rugby, math team, debate team and he excelled in everything. His father wanted to expand his experiences so Ricardo was sent to college in America. There, he changed to his American name, spoke mostly English and became the Richard we know now."

Mychal knew her husband went to

college in Miami but she had no idea he was an undercover nerd. She asked, "Was he named after you? Is that where he met that psychopath?"

His uncle laughed in a hardy baritone, "Yes he is named after me and no, he met her later when he moved back home. But he had his share of girlfriends before her, each a model, actress or professional athlete. He had his heart broken a few times because he was always in love with the idea of romance. When his father and I would fly to the states, he would either be love struck or depressed after a breakup. Richard wanted to come home right after finishing his second degree but his parents wanted him to stay and enjoy life outside of the area. He played minor league soccer for a few years while enjoying the Miami nightlife."

Uncle Rico paused with a sigh then said, "That was before my best friend got sick. Richard was homesick anyway so when he heard his father was in the hospital he came home to stay. He and Alejandra nursed Rohas back to health with Richard stepping in to take the business reigns. The twins were busy teenagers and Richard also helped with them. Then he started dating that Greek girl. He met her a few times at theater parties and fell for her. She was a little older than him and used him as a play toy to advance her career. His parents hated her, so he only saw her when she was in town. When the twins were finishing their last year of *Bachillerato*, Alejandra was in a car accident and never fully recovered despite the family's efforts. In a debilitated state, she died and less than two years later my best friend Rohas died too. I think he could not live without her."

"The children were devastated but had each other for support. Richard was already running the company and threw himself into work as a way to deal with his grief. That Greek girl came back into his life with a vengeance knowing how lost and hurt he was without his parents. She controlled his entire life from the way he dressed to where they ate. He wanted children and she convinced him they would have just one eventually, when she was ready. She knew what to say to keep him in place. And everything was for publicity, especially their high profile engagement. I saw more of Richard in the entertainment news than I saw him in person. As she pulled him away from the business, it suffered."

"When Richard realized his father's namesake was failing, he immediately spent the time needed to save it. That meant dividing his time between work, family, and his relationship. She was livid not being his number one priority. For a while he tried to make things work, but at the cost of his health. Then unable to maintain that level of stress by stretching himself beyond his limits, he broke it off causing her to lose her mind. After wreaking havoc and almost having him arrested, things mellowed out between them. He tried to remain friendly out of obligation. Then along came you, the best thing he ever had that he was smart enough to keep."

Mychal blushed and said, "Thank you Uncle Rico, but really he was the best thing that ever happened to me. I love him so much."

The older gentleman got up and she rose too, "My dear that is all you two need. We are done for the day. Take my beautiful great niece home and enjoy the rest of your day."

Impulsively she hugged him again, "Thank you for everything Uncle Rico."

He hugged back relaying it was his pleasure.

Feeling better than she had in almost a year, Mychal collected her sleeping daughter and went home.

Richard and Evan were having coffee at an outside café. Both were dressed casual at the moment with Richard in sandals, jeans and a college t-shirt and Evan in flip flops, cargo shorts and a navy blue Baja with a surf shop logo. Even though he was not in the office, he still had his shoulder length sun bleached caramel colored hair in a ponytail. To the average layman it looked like two guys watching an event on a tablet, but they were actually conversing with a private detective.

Richard believed the authorities were doing their best, which to him was not good enough. One accomplice dead, one missing and a hidden flash drive was leaving everybody with no answers. Evan did his homework and found a super discrete person to do the job they needed. So discrete that Richard was not sure if the person on the video link was a man or a woman. Whoever it was, despite the cloak and dagger, was pretty damn good. The person already had a file developed on the dead accomplice that included everything from his ex-wives to his local grocery shopping market. Richard was beyond pleased. The video chat was to setup a method of payment and any other specific modifications to the investigation Richard had in mind.

After tossing around ideas with the investigator, he and Evan had a clear understanding of the direction the investigation would take with the end result of turning everything legal over to the authorities to help with their case. Terminating the link, their next item on the agenda was the status of the hacker or new company IT consultant which was how Richard was justifying the company expense.

The flash drive had an encryption code that the hacker easily broke, but the information on the drive was confusing. It was a list of answered ads from a website, some scanned documents and pictures. The pictures were of houses, cars and people in compromising positions. Richard made a note to review them later. The documents were a list of companies and their holdings in off shore accounts. The ads were written in Russian, which none of them could read. Feeling they were inching closer to a key piece of information, Richard gave Evan the green light to keep pursuing the matter further. Evan made the comment the more information they had, the less they actually knew. Richard agreed.

On his way home Richard contacted Max. The lawyer picked up the phone with, "How are things in beautiful Madrid?"

"They are fine and New York?"

"Rainy. I'm hanging around the office until after rush hour traffic."

"Good plan. Do you have a

minute?"

"Yeah anytime. What's up?"

"How much money will it take to solve the mess with Riley's husband?"

Max chuckled, "I wish it was as easy as writing a check. Jacob is in a lot of trouble and he's too stupid to take a plea deal. He is hoping to sway a judge but the facts in his case don't lie."

"What will happen to Riley?"

"I don't know. She needs to go back to work. Right now she is just depressed because she does not know what to do. Ma, Reese, Mychal and I are supporting her emotionally and financially. When Jake goes to prison, she will be lost."

Richard chose his words carefully, "Jake sounds like a prideful man. Which do you think he loves more, his wife or his pride?"

Max was silent at first before joking, "That's a strange question with mysterious undertones."

"Based on the situation surrounding Riley's husband he likes money but does not want to work honestly for it. He wanted to take care of Riley because he put the money in things for them. So if he loves her, then perhaps he will accept a plea deal for a less amount of time so he will not spend the majority of his adult life away from his wife," Richard rationalized.

Max liked Richard's insight. He had approached the situation like a lawyer but his brother-in-law's angle was that of a business man. "I think that idea should be brought up with both Riley and Jacob. Let me call Jake's lawyer to see what the prosecutor's office might offer."

"I will talk to Mychal on my end. She may not have the best influence with Riley but she does have leverage." Richard had a thought and said, "I do not want you to think I am trying to use the housing situation to influence Riley. With all that being said, I need her to realize that the adults in her life cannot support her like a teenager or like her husband has done in the past."

"Agreed. It seems this situation might force my baby sister to finally grow up," Max sighed.

Richard smiled, "Adversity will do that."

He waited until later that evening to approach the subject with Mychal. She was reading to Carrigan when he came into the nursery. Richard loved to hear Mychal read because she gave each character a different voice. She was reading about wishing stars and sheep as the baby chewed her own fingers. Mychal looked up and smiled, but kept reading. When she was done, she gave the sleepy infant her pacifier and put her in the crib. Richard came in to kiss his daughter goodnight and put on her lullaby projector. It lit up the ceiling with stars while playing soft music. Mychal eased out with him right behind her.

While she showered, Richard brushed his teeth and talked. "I know you are helping Riley. Just how much is your family financially supporting her?"

From the shower she said, "You knew already we were her sole support. She is living in my mother's house rent free."

"Do you send her money?"

The shower cut off, "Not really. I am helping my mom who I know is helping Riley."

Richard waited until they were in bed to tell her about his idea for Jacob to accept a plea deal to help her sister.

Mychal dismissed his suggestion immediately, "That selfish bastard loves himself more than he loves my sister."

"*Bella*," Richard rubbed her arm, "I know what he is and it is his very nature that I am betting on. His selfishness is what Riley can appeal to, that is, if she is willing to work it out so they can still have a life together."

She looked at him and half joked, "What are you planning, you evil genius?"

Richard gave her a vampire laugh as he pulled Mychal into his arms to nibble on her neck, "Come and find out."

6
Sisters and Disputes

Mychal had the suspicion that Susanna was avoiding her. She came to the house to visit during the week but did not stay very long. Richard told Mychal that his sister was busy with her business proposal and school. His wife would not take that answer as satisfactory so she made a point to visit early one Thursday morning. Susanna came to the door with bed head and crusty eyes. "Mychal, what's wrong?"

"Nothing, I came to visit and have coffee with warm bagels," she held up the bag.

"You do know what time it is?"

Mychal smiled, "Of course I do. Did I wake Javier or were you two . . ."

"It's too early for comedy," Susanna smiled.

"True but I'm not leaving until I have coffee. I pumped this morning so now I can enjoy a good cup of decaf."

"Is mine decaf too?"

"Yes, why should I suffer alone. If I can't get a decent cup of joe you can't either," Mychal tried to explain. She saw her sister-in-law was not following her American reference, "A cup of joe, coffee. Aw hell, just go tell Javier it's not an intruder and meet me in your kitchen."

For close to an hour the two women talked about things going on in their lives. Mychal told Susanna about Richard's plan to get her brother-in-law to accept a plea deal. Susanna talked about her business

143

plan that Tony was helping her write since he was now taking business classes. She did not mention her progress on the wedding plans so Mychal brought it up.

"They are moving right along," was all Susanna would say.

Mychal made a face, "So you did **not** talk to your brother about **not** wanting some big wedding yet?"

"I tried," the younger woman threw up her hands, "but he said to pick a date and it would be a small lavish event with no business associates. We have two hundred people between friends and family. He never listens."

"You do know your brother."

"The more I hear about setting a date, the more I want to elope. Javé works around the socially elite snobs all the time and he nor I really want to share our special day with them." Susanna paused then said, "I also have been thinking about asking

144

Javé to move in permanently first. I have always lived in the house with family and various staff members. That is so outdated. I want to live like people my age who reside with boyfriends in the current century."

Mychal finally understood. She felt like she needed to step in to help so she said, "I think my husband needs to respect your wishes. While I will not directly intervene, I will remind him that your day is a special day, not an opportunity for business or family affairs. That is unless you and Javier want it to be. I love Richard very much and am aware that at times his business sense and his common sense do not work well together."

Susanna chewed her lip so Mychal asked, "What's wrong?"

"I wonder should I send Javier to have this conversation with Richard."

Mychal got up to leave, "You two

talk it over and whatever you decide, I will support you."

"Thanks. Kiss my niece."

"I will," she waved as she walked out the door.

Mychal really wanted to talk with Richard about leaving his sister to her own vices. She held it in for two days before approaching him. They were in the kitchen making a grocery list while Carrigan scooted around the floor in her walker chasing the dog.

"Honey can I bring something up and you won't get mad?"

He looked and said, "Funny, I was about to ask you the same thing."

"Why?"

"Because I know you usually talk with your family on Sundays and I need you to bring up my idea to Riley."

She was clearly not expecting that subject matter. Mychal was reluctant to even bring up the plea deal because her sister was so sensitive about everything lately. So she put it back on Richard. "I thought it would be better received coming from you."

Richard started, "I do not really know her like that- "

"So," Mychal sharply cut him off, "you know her well enough to talk to her. Why do I have to be in the middle?"

He was quite taken back by her sudden attitude shift. He asked, "Has anything changed since we last talked about this?"

"No," Mychal huffed then switched her tone, "I'm sorry. I am just so damn tired of this. . . this foolishness. All of my life I have lived with the messiness of Riley's pettiness and poor decisions. This is just another event in the long running saga of my sister and her train wreck of a life causing casualties to those around her. Even when I don't have to testify anymore, or so I hope, somehow this chaos continues to affect me a whole country away."

"That is because you let it," he sighed.

"Richard please! You can't even say anything to me about letting family stuff bother somebody. Your sister is trying to plan her own wedding but is crippled by your constant intrusiveness."

"What!"

Mychal wished she could take back the last part but the proverbial cat was out of the bag. She inwardly sighed but said "You let stuff about Tony and Susanna, especially Susanna, bother you all the time. 'Bella, she wants to quit school'. 'She wants to marry someone who is not an oil prince'. 'She wants to join the circus'. You always complain about your siblings and have to be reminded to stay in your lane. I am just tired of my sister and her draining drama that never seems to stop. Day in and day out the problems of Riley and her dumbass husband hang over my head like a storm cloud waiting to ruin any measure of happiness in my life. I have reached the end of my rope with her and you are acting like I have the problem. She has done enough in all of our lives and dammit I am sick of it!"

The room was quiet and tense. Richard's mouth was a tight line and Mychal's eyes blazed with raw emotion. Even the baby and dog looked at them. Finally, Richard got up and walked to leave the room, eyes reflecting his own emotions, mostly hurt. Seeing the damage she caused, Mychal caught him, "Honey, I'm sorry."

He made a motion to pull away but Mychal would not let him go. "Honey, please. Please talk to me. I had no right to take things out on you. Richard, I love you and I know you are just trying to make things better."

His eyes softened a little and he said, "I am not your enemy *Bella*."

"I know and I hate it when we fight," she felt guilty as she wiped away a tear. "To be honest I hate talking to Riley at this point. She is so damn selfish that I just can't take her attitude anymore. She's so fuc- "

"Hey, hey, baby and dog in the room."

Suddenly Mychal was physically tired. Tired of the current conversation, tired of fighting with Richard, and tired of the mess she was in. Unconsciously her shoulders sagged and she said, "I need some air."

"I think we both need some air. I will take Carrigan out for a stroll. You take some time to yourself then maybe see if Solomon needs a walk," Richard picked up

150

the baby and walked outside.

Twenty minutes later, she had a glass of wine and a tennis ball. She and the dog joined Richard and the baby outside. Solomon found them in the flower garden in Mychal's favorite spot. Richard was talking to his daughter about how his mother loved flowers and how she would work all summer with Papa Pedro to get the garden prepared for parties. His voice calmed Mychal so much. He loved her like no other person in life had ever loved her. As much as she hated to do it, she would call her sister tonight. Mychal walked over and kissed his hair, "I love you. I'm sorry for being testy ."

"These are difficult times. Believe me, I understand but again I need you to recognize that I am not your enemy," he punctuated the last five words for extra emphasis.

"I know. You are my best friend in the whole world."

"Do not tell Max that, he has been your best friend all your life."

Mychal noted how he cleverly picked up on that fact, "Who is your best friend? Wait, I know . . . Uncle Rico."

Richard was surprised, "How did you guess?"

"He told me some stories I'm sure your father did not know."

He chuckled, "Uncle Rico has been more than my godfather; he was truly my best friend. That was until you."

"I can share. I love him like he was one of my own uncles."

"And he loves you."

Taking a breath she said, "I will talk with Riley tonight."

"You do not have to because of me," he sounded skeptical.

"No, I will because of us. Max once said we deserve a life. If getting peace in our lives means talking my sister into a smart decision, then that is what I will do."

"Whatever you think will work. I was once told happy wife, happy life."

Mychal rolled her eyes, "Let me guess, your best friend told you that"

Richard smiled.

Talking to her sister required something stronger than wine. While Richard put the baby to bed, Mychal logged in on her laptop for a video chat with Riley. When she came on the screen, Mychal tried to keep everything light, "What's up sis?"

"Same old, same old."

They made light chit chat about their mother and home. They talked about their brothers before Riley mentioned Max talking to Jacob. Mychal inquired was there anything new. Her sister's attitude quickly changed when she said Max wanted Jake to take a plea deal.

"And?"

Riley exploded, "And he should not take anything because he is innocent! I don't want to lose my husband if he didn't do anything wrong."

Mychal took a sip of her drink and a breath, "Riley, you knew there was a problem. Whether you knew then how he got the money or not, you know now. I am not questioning any of the how we got to this point, as I am trying to figure out what to do next."

On the screen her sister crossed her arms and said, "So you are convinced he's guilty?"

"Riley, we are not the ones that need convincing of his guilt or innocence," Richard spoke up behind his wife. She was so incensed Mychal never even heard him come in the room. He had the baby who was rubbing her eyes. Richard bent down so Riley could see them both.

On the screen Riley's demeanor changed. Her anger was replaced with instant silliness. She said, "Who's that girl? Is that auntie's snuggle bug?"

Carrigan broke out smiling, dropping her pacifier, drooling and making baby noises. Richard moved her in front of the camera. Riley's voice seemed to encourage her more as she said, "Look at that big girl. What are you still doing up? Are you going to keep your mommy and daddy up all night? You need to go to sleep snuggle bug."

The infant made her own babbling conversation noises at her aunt's silly voice. Richard looked at Mychal and winked. She looked back perplexed. With his eyes he looked over to the bed as if to say, 'go over there'. He did it again and when she finally got his meaning, left the chair. Richard sat in the chair and held Carrigan while Riley made silly faces and talked. When she began to whine, he gave her the pacifier and talked to Riley. Feeling relieved her part was over, Mychal went to take a shower. When she got out Richard was holding a sleeping Carrigan and laughing with Riley.

"Hey sis," she said from the monitor, "you didn't tell me about your big plans. Have fun."

Mychal stood behind Richard and flashed a fake smile. Her sister burst into laughter while he just smiled too. "I know you two got stuff to work on. I love you both. Kiss my niece. Richard, I'll be in touch. Bye sis,"

Her sister disconnected the chat.

Utterly confused, Mychal looked at Richard, who just grinned, super pleased with himself.

"What was that about? What did you do and what did you say?"

"Nothing."

She went to gently pick up the sleeping baby, "Well I want an answer to nothing after I put her down."

When she came back from settling the baby for the night, Richard was already in bed waiting for her and wearing that same sly smile. She climbed into bed, "Spill it."

"It is nothing, really. I just got Riley to agree that a plea deal would work for her future with Jacob."

Mychal frowned, "How did you do that? Appeal to her selfish nature?"

"Why yes, and thanks to our daughter," he ignored his wife's dirty look. "*Bella*, you and your sister still have some unresolved issues. Not a lot, but enough that she often reverts back to her feelings in certain situations. She believes you still have a superior attitude when it comes to her life."

"You know I don't give a damn about- "

Richard cut her off, "I know that but she is entitled to her feelings, especially now. So, I used her feelings as a platform to show her how she can still have her dreams as well as avoid the judgment she might receive from you and others as the trial progresses."

Mychal felt her anger ebbing, "So is she going to convince her sorry ass husband to go for a plea deal or just telling you what you want to hear?"

"Carrigan convinced her that she should advise Jacob to take a deal that will give her cousins and enjoy growing old with her husband."

"Yuck. I can't even think of her having kids with that bastard. How did my child convince her they should ever conceive?"

"*Bella simplemente parar*. Put aside

158

your anger toward the situation and look at the fact your sister deserves some happiness for what he has put her through as well." When she did not have a snappy comeback, Richard knew his words found their target. "You are not looking at anything from Riley's viewpoint. Her siblings are successful with their own families and her one shot at having the same looks so bleak that she might be alone for twenty years before she will ever see her husband again. That is how I got Riley to understand the plea deal was best for not just him, but also for them as a married couple. I see the way she loves to interact with Carrigan. Riley wants a family too."

Mychal was suddenly overcome with a wave of sadness for her sister. The back of her eyes suddenly moistened

"So you see, helping her look at the situation in shorter terms made the end result seem a little more bearable. That and making her see she has to get her household ready if she wants a family.

Riley liked being taken care of, but after we talked she understood that tragedies can happen anytime. I proposed what ifs to her as in what if Jacob was paralyzed in an accident, what if they had a family and he had no career. Then what would she do? The same thing she needs to do now, step up to the challenge and do what needs to be done to survive."

Mychal was speechless. Richard had really thrown her sister in the deep end of the truth pool, "And she said?"

"And I think she got the message. She said she would get a job and her own place as soon as she got a steady paycheck. I told her we would help by continuing to let your mother stay at your house, but Riley would pay her own utilities and upkeep of your mother's home. Tia is on a fixed income and should not have to worry about taking care of herself and her grown children. Your sister would save her rent money and have enough to get an apartment when the time comes. I said we would help as much as we could for a limited time, emphasis on a limited time. But I insisted she needed to work on her own independence so we could work on things here."

"Things like?"

Richard took her hand and slid it under the sheets where he was naked. "Like our own growing family."

"Oh, that's what you have been smiling about."

This time the smile was a wolfish grin that conveyed no good intentions. He pulled Mychal into his arms for a hungry yet passionate kiss. Her body responded as if it were their first night together; the way she responded every time he touched her in a seductive way. Mychal was feeling mischievous. She broke their kiss to trail more kisses down his chest. Richard's breath caught as she flicked his nipples with her tongue. She continued down to his tapered waist until she reached the spot her hand had been previously. With an equally impish smile and wink, Mychal showed her intent to please and tease him with her tongue and lips.

Richard was aroused by her provocative flirting and senses scrambled by her actions. She was weakening his self-control with every flick of her tongue.

"*Bella*, please. I . . . cannot . . . "

"Then don't," she enticed him with a naughty grin.

Richard let go in the comfort of her supple breast. Her boldness and sensuous invitation was such a turn on, "Bella, I need to feel you."

With the skill of a gymnast she straddled him then eased onto him. Mychal leaned over to brush her bare slick breast against his chest and whispered in his ear, "Is that all you got?"

"*Dios mio!*" Richard bear hugged her to roll them over, pushing her knees against his shoulders. With passionate urgency, he pushed them over the edge into ecstasy. Afterward as he lay holding her, neither said a word. Just when Mychal started to move thinking he was sleep, Richard said, "Oh, I am nowhere close to sleep. Where do you think you are going?"

She could feel his desire rising again. "As a matter of fact, I was just thinking of trying something else new."

"Oh?"

Richard withdrew and turned Mychal onto her stomach, "Yes Bella. You cannot touch me but I can touch you. Anyway I want."

Mychal was a little unsure until she felt his light kiss in the small of her back. Her whole body shivered in anticipative response and she moaned. "I think I'm going to like this."

Richard moved up to press himself between her thighs and whispered in her ear, "Trust me, you are going to love this."

7

Lawyers and Developments

"Mr. Otulinboson has called several times and left messages for you to call back," Richard's personal assistant, Morcheeba, interrupted his thoughts as he walked by her desk on his way to Tony's office.

Otulinboson. Otulinboson. The name sounded strange yet familiar even with Morcheeba's heavy Rwandan accent. "I do not recognize the name."

"He called on line seven so you must know him somehow."

That struck Richard as odd. Line

seven was his secure line and he knew most of the people that would have that number. Mentally waving off the confusion, he asked about Morcheeba's brothers, Kendo and Kumova. She happily switched the subject to talk about how well one was doing in school and the other was excelling in sports.

Richard smiled at the boys' progress. He remembered the day his father got the call there were refugees found on board the ship. He came home and told the story to the family. There were three boys, all were under the age of ten, with one being a toddler. No one had any idea where they came from or how they survived the trip. Out on the docks the three ebony skinned boys huddled together, the oldest trying to quiet the whining toddler. The ship's captain was furious and the dock workers were uneasy.

Later relaying the events to his family, Rohas told them that when he saw that the ragged, weary and frightened

166

children that his heart just broke. They were malnourished and dressed in tattered filthy clothing. Their sunken faces were dirty and marked with tear streaks and their limbs covered with open sores. His father said when he approached them, they huddled together more. He tried to speak with them in Spanish, French, Arabic, and Portuguese with no luck. Then his father asked did they need food in English. The oldest one said yes too fast, letting on they knew some English. Rohas sent a worker to get sandwiches from a vendor close to the docks.

As the children wolfed down the food, they talked very little to the stranger that provided their meal. But he managed to get their family was trying to escape the Rwanda Genocide, the result of the Hutu and Tutsi Civil War. Many of their family members were killed in front of them and they had no idea if their mother or father were alive. The oldest remaining child was put in charge of the younger two and somehow snuck all three on the first ship they came to on the waterway. They survived by stealing food and catching bugs to eat. Their story brought the Garçia-Torrés patriarch to tears. He called his trusted friend and lawyer Rico to help the children.

After getting his private physician to check the children out, something new came to light, the oldest boy was really a girl. Richard's father rallied his family to find the children some assistance. His father's oldest brother and his wife stepped forward to care for the three and eventually adopted them. Richard grew up with Morcheeba and her brothers as first cousins. She was more than his personal assistant, she was the trusted face of family in a business where there was so little to trust.

"Earth to Ricardo. Where were you just then, back with Mychal?" Morcheeba teased.

"Jokes? You are too funny today," he shot back on his way to Tony's office. He walked in on his brother eating lunch and the office smelling of a light perfume. Richard smiled, "Where's Yadira?"

"She left about ten minutes ago. She brought me lunch and possibly dinner."

"I did not get any special lunch."

"No you did not. Brother when are you going to use contractions, slang, or any dialect in the current decade? You sound old and regal like Papa. I would never guess you spent all those years in America."

"I do not-" Richard caught himself. He smiled and said, "I don't sound old and I didn't get any special lunch."

"It's a start. She made enough. I told her I might be working late, so she added extra for dinner."

"You sure?"

"Help yourself," Tony slid the container and extra plate to Richard.

Richard was hungry. While eating he talked to Tony about the possibility of a new human resources company. He needed one that might also subcontract for Evan's new security team. Tony threw out the idea of marketing the contract to a Canadian business to add any customers that company might already have which would create more revenue. The company he had in mind mostly dealt with South America and the eastern regions of North America. With an opening in the Canadian market, they could move up the east coast to pick up contracts as well. Tony had a solid plan with far reaching potential.

Richard's phone buzzed with a text from Evan requesting a meeting in the next hour. He replied that he would be in Evan's office in thirty minutes. Richard continued talking with his brother about his classes and Yadira. Tony discussed Susanna and Javier's creeping to a halt wedding plans, causing Richard to frown. Richard told him Mychal suggested he back off their plans. Tony just commented that Mychal would not have said anything to him without a reason. Richard made a sour face and left for Evan's office.

Once he entered the office closest to the stairs, Evan closed the door and turned on his TV. Richard gave him the 'what the hell' look. Evan handed him a thick folder. "You know the encryption on the files was broken. That is what was found."

Richard opened the folder which had at least a hundred pages. He leafed through shipping manifests, pictures of the dock, and bank statements, "Some of this I recognize, but am I missing something?"

"You are not but you just need to keep going. In the back there are over lapping direct deposits from the current human resources company to Salamanca and from another company called the Adonis Arts Foundation. While that company does charity work for the elderly in third world areas, it does not answer why it was paying Salamanca large monthly sums. So I had my hacker dig deeper. The major shareholder is a shell corporation that is owned by some global corporation with ties in Turkey, Brazil, Greece and England.

"So, some big conglomerate is behind trying to sabotage my company?" Richard was more annoyed than before. "And Evan, what the hell is up with the TV and why is it so loud?"

"Richard, that guy had surveillance on a few people. How did he get the shipping manifest and pictures of everybody? You need to look more closely. There are pictures of all of us including Mychal, Morcheeba and Tony's car after the accident."

Richard immediately went back to the pictures. There were at least a dozen pictures each of ten people, most of which he knew. Evan, Tony, Susanna, Morcheeba, his union rep, the ship's captain, himself, and some dock workers he only recognized from their uniform. The last four pictures were disturbing and strange. One was of Mychal in the university parking lot and two were of Demitri in two different situations. In one she was leaving the parking garage with containers similar to paint cans and in the other she was on the lot of a rental car company. The last picture was of Rafael and an older gentleman that Richard did not immediately recognize but thought looked familiar.

"So," Evan broke his thoughts, "someone has been watching us and I have a theory. Salamanca was the one or one of the ones that started the dock incidents. I say one of the ones because this guy was not your typical muscle for hire. He was smart. All these additional documents were from him doing research on his employer. The fact it was hidden on that jump drive let me know he did *not* trust his employer and needed insurance from the worst case scenario. Both the shipping manifest and the pictures gave hints to the dates. In the pictures, Mychal was not really looking pregnant so that dates maybe early spring. The shipping manifests started out with everything, but by summer only targeted a few ports. So he did extensive planning."

"I see. Do you think we have a mole in the company?" Richard was growing concerned.

"No, but there is a chance that we might be under surveillance at any moment by the other accomplice. I just gave you the evidence that we were being watched at one point." Evan saw the boss man's face change. "Wait, before you go off and pull the fire alarm, I got this. Tonight I'm having the hacker come in and check our computers. I also purchased a frequency detector and will sweep the offices while he is here. That thing was not cheap, so do not come down here later like I surprised you with an item that blew my entire equipment budget."

"Thanks for the heads up."

"*Su nada*. I also used the fringe account to acquire a top of the line lock pick gun "

"What is that? Never mind. With you I have learned to ask fewer questions."

Evan smiled, "You finally learned *jefé*."

Richard went on to share with Evan the fact that he decided to give him a security team and wanted to change human resource companies. Evan agreed to both and added he needed to keep his computer hacker on for company cyber security purposes. Richard approved. Before leaving he asked Evan if he should be playing music while working, just in case they were under surveillance at the moment.

Evan laughed, "Maybe, because if you like the same music as your wife, someone listening will mistake you for a teenager at a rave party and stop recording anything you say."

"Who told you that? Tony?"

"Yep, your wife is certainly different."

"Yes she is."

Sunday afternoon Richard decided to grill out. He invited Ruby and Luis over for a day at the pool and to discuss being Carrigan's godparents. The couple was delighted and spent most of their time playing with the infant. After dinner, they sat around the stone fire pit and discussed current events as everyone was so preoccupied with their own lives.

Luis and Ruby were planning to visit their daughter in Cairo at the end of the semester. Tony was working on his degree while dating Yadira. Susanna was busy with school, starting her non-profit and working toward being Mrs. Javier. Richard was planning to expand the company and Mychal was deep into thesis committees. Now that Ruby and Luis were going to be godparents, it was time to plan Carrigan's christening.

Mychal groaned inside, but did not let Richard know. He was such a traditional guy that if she objected to some formal ceremony, he would be upset. Growing up her family were not devote church goers. However, they went to services occasionally and on Christian holidays. As a teenager she got a job that included working on some weekends and relegating church to just holidays. Mychal considered herself as having a strong spiritual foundation, which in her eyes did not require regular church attendance. Richard on the other hand was more devoted to his religion and occasionally went to church without her. The idea sparked in Mychal's mind that the christening might be a chance to see her family. If that was the case, she would be on board for whatever Richard wanted.

Mychal tried to catch Susanna home for the next week but was unsuccessful. Saturday morning she went by the apartment early enough to wake Susanna up.

"Mychal," she answered the door disheveled, "is something wrong?"

"No, I have been trying to reach you. I texted and came by, but no answer. The better question is, are you alright?"

Susanna looked at her sister-in-law more alert. Mychal looked like she was not going anywhere until she got answers. "Come in but ignore the mess."

Mychal walked into the apartment to

see piles of paper all over the living room. Susanna plopped on the couch while Mychal sat on the cleanest chair. "So, this is . . . what?"

"The planning of the next stage of my life," Susanna sighed. With help from Papa Plasencia and Uncle Rico she had a business plan for her music therapy company. She already had information on various locations that had dwelling space to live or expand into an office.

"What are your brothers going to think of that? You possibly moving out."

Susanna shrugged and commented in a few months that would be a decision for her and Javier, her new husband. She went on to explain to Mychal that in her research most proprietors had advance degrees, so she was applying to graduate programs in rehabilitation therapy and investigating vocational schools that offered training.

179

Mychal was mildly surprised and now understood why the other woman was incommunicado. Then she said, "I don't hear much wedding planning."

Susanna made a sour face so she said in a softer tone, "Have you talked to your brother about toning down your day?"

"No, I have been beyond busy. I barely found time to hang out with everybody by the pool last week."

Mychal sat silently while the wheels turned in her head. Susanna did not even sound excited about getting married anymore. Instead she asked, "When are you graduating?"

"Next summer session or fall. Why?"

"Just wondering could you down play the wedding with a graduation celebration."

"Not on my brother's watch. He

threw a lawn party just to court clients. That and to celebrate Demitri being caught and jailed."

Mychal smiled at her husband's business smarts, "He does like to party. All he needs is a sound business reason."

"True," Susanna huffed, "like all those university galas. It was fun, but it brought in big money for scholarships and projects from all the wallets of people meaning alumni, community business, investors looking for write offs and his owns business associates."

"Too bad you can't use those same people for your new venture.

Susanna smiled as an idea suddenly spouted in her mind, "Maybe."

Susanna made a point to go see Richard on her way home from class the next week. He was leaving the office so she was able to convince him they should talk over tapas and drinks. First he checked with his wife, then agreed. They went to a small bar near The Plaza Mayor and sat outside to talk.

"*Así hermana*, what is new in your life? We both have been so busy we need to play catch up."

"Indeed, but I thought Mychal would have talked to you by now."

Richard smiled, "My wife has reminded me that she quit being the Susanna interpreter a while ago. Then she proclaimed that she will no longer be an unpaid mediator between family members. So I need all the details of what's going on and leave nothing out."

Susanna talked to her brother about starting her own business and working with Uncle Rico on her business plans. She tied that into her first bombshell of the evening, needing additional education to have the knowledge of how to merge the two disciplines. So a graduate degree in rehabilitation or vocational counseling with a few courses in business was in her plan. "What do you think so far?"

All he said was, "Continue."

Susanna continued with her timeline of career growth and business growth. She began talking about wanting to have a large event to introduce her business when Richard interrupted her.

"All this talk has been about business. When are we going to talk about your wedding?"

Susanna made a face and sighed, "Alright, this is the deal. Javier does not care for being the center of attention. He is very shy and only on board for a large wedding if I want that. But this man is about to be my partner and husband and I must consider his feelings."

Quietly, Richard asked, "What do

you want?"

"I want my business to take off. I was never crazy about a big affair that was all about me and Javé. I told you that I was over the recital display mentality when Mama and Papa died. As I started the business planning, I realized I wanted the spotlight to be less on me and more on the cause. I really feel like some big affair that requires money and attention should be a benefit to someone somewhere else. A large wedding should not have a payoff to us as we are already behaving in the capacity of a married couple." Susanna paused, then finished with, "I would rather have my passion receive the financial gains."

Richard was quiet in his own thoughts. He gave his sister a slow smile then said, "*Mi hermanita ya no es un bebé.*"

"*Dios mio!*"

"No seriously, I am proud of you,"

Richard tried to explain, "You have grown so much in a short amount of time. Who knew my sweet little sister had the business mind of a shark?"

Susanna smiled back with pride.

Richard covered her hand with his, "Whatever you want I will support."

She squeezed his hand, "*Gracias hermano*. I knew you would understand."

"So, when is the wedding? Since as you say, you are already living like a married couple."

"We will let you know. I will give you a seven day notice.

"Funny, but that's not going to work. At least have the immediate family and a dinner." When Susanna did not come back with her usual quip, Richard said, "Okay, what is really going on? I watched you help plan my own wedding. I remember you saying things like wanting your wedding colors to be the color of the ocean and evening clouds and how you wanted mama's favorite flowers in your bouquet. I know something else is at play here. You might as well come clean because I will not let this go."

Susanna sighed with resignation, knowing her brother. "You are right and I see you are not going to let this go. But if I tell you, you cannot tell Javier I said a word."

"You are my sister. My loyalties are always with you."

"Papa Plasençia took Javier from an orphanage and raised him. When Javier's mother died, his father put him in that place to neatly hide the product of his secret extra marital affair. His father is somebody important in government and has limited contact with Javé ."

"I see," Richard was beginning to understand.

"Javier thinks his real father might try to use our marriage to some political advantage."

Her brother squeezed and patted her hand, "Well Javier is part of our family now. I will not let anybody use him or you. I want happiness for both of you, so we will do something intimate for just family and then introduce your company in whatever fashion you like."

Susanna felt a weight was finally lifted. She squeezed Richard's hand back, "Thank you for understanding."

He smiled back, "For you, anything."

8
Motivations and Meetings

It might have taken Richard a considerable amount of time to accept Susanna's small wedding idea if Mychal had not discouraged his waning attitude about the matter. One minute he was pouting and commenting on how Susanna should at least have a moderate closed wedding. The next minute, he was proud of her accomplishments and looked forward to her company's introduction, slash, reception party.

His temperate attitude went on for almost two weeks before Susanna gave Mychal the date she and Javier picked out.

Mychal was as happy for the soon to be married couple as a measure of tranquility would hopefully return to her world. She even went a step further and suggested Susanna hire an event planner for her combination reception and company inauguration celebration. Mychal felt slightly guilty about her motivations but she could not help her sister-in-law the way Susanna helped with her wedding. Mychal wanted her to understand the circumstances were different but the end results were the same. She would support Susanna any way she could between teaching, Carrigan and keeping Richard off the emotional ledge.

Mychal could see his stress level seemed to be somewhat improving. He more freely talked about the progress in the sabotage situation at night as they relaxed in bed. Richard made it his goal to keep his wife informed of everything, just not involved.

Tony's decision to go to school was not an easy one for him, but it was motivated by a combination of personal and professional reasons. He felt an overwhelming pressure to be something more than what he currently was because his twin was a musical genius and his older brother a business mastermind. Growing up Tony always felt like he was never enough when it came to measuring up to his siblings. Richard was his parents' first born and excelled at everything they expected from him. He was outstanding in school, involved in the community and a great athlete.

Susanna was the only girl and a miniature version of their grandmother, who introduced her to the piano at the age of four. When they visited their grandparents in the country, their Abeulita would sing while their Abeulito played the guitar. After she mastered the piano,

Susanna moved to learning the guitar and played with him. Tony would watch, wondering if he would ever be special like that to do special things with their grandparents.

When their grandparents had to be cared for and his parents had the apartment built for them, Tony would spend his time listening to his grandfather's stories of the times before he met their grandmother. He would tell the young Antonio about the world and fill his imagination with stories of West Indian and English merchants coming to the tavern where he worked. He always ended the stories with how Abeulita came to sing on Saturday nights and eventually they fell in love. Tony took his grandparents' passing harder than the others because Abeulito was like a best friend.

Growing up Tony tried to do everything his older brother would do. He tried sports but was never in any starting positions like Richard. He tried to learn an instrument but the only thing he was decent at was the drums, which like everything else, his parents tolerated. The only thing he really excelled at was trying anything new and his parents' patience at every turn. He was always doing this to get his parents' attention. He concentrated on ways to outsmart his parents and siblings. If Susanna got money for good grades, Tony would make her feel bad enough to share it with him. If his parents grounded him, he would enroll in a school community service project to get out of the house.

When his father got sick, Rohas told Tony that he needed him to grow up and do better in school. Papa loved hearing how his day was at school. At bed time, Tony would read to his father before going to bed or fall asleep on his bed. While their father recovered from his illness, Richard was back in the house being the perfect son again. Again, Tony returned to his old ways, however this time he was beginning

high school and girls were his new interest.
He went through girls like water, much to
his parents' dismay. To keep them off his
back, Tony became an above average
student whose popularity grew.

When their mother got in a car
accident that almost ended her life, Tony's
world changed. Though a teenager, Tony
pitched in to help care for his mother. He
hid his pain of watching her waste away
with partying and girls. His heart broke
twice in less than eighteen months, first his
mother passed and then his father. He and
his siblings mourned together, but he
veiled his pain in a string of women and
endless partying. While his brother was
lost in Demitri, Tony was lost in a series of
empty, shallow, and pointless relationships.
He was reckless and careless, manipulating
women and disrespecting households, even
his own.

His first wakeup call came after the
husband of some one night stand tried to
shoot him. The secondary was when

Richard's control crazed girlfriend totaled his truck, then tried to have him arrested through false accusations. That is when Tony realized that he might lose his brother and he would have to guide Susanna as family patriarch.

As the family licked its proverbial wounds after that debacle, Mychal crashed into their lives, starting a chain of events that led him to meet the best thing in his life, Yadira. She was like no one he had ever dated and after the car accident, Tony knew he was a changed man. Not only did he want to change for her, but he also wanted to become a company asset and overall better man. He wanted to replace the old Tony, the playboy, with a newer, serious and educated Tony, the vice president.

Tony had a presentation due at midnight. He worked on it as much as he could at his desk, but needed some resources at home. After letting Morcheeba know his afternoon plans, he headed to the car. As he walked across the parking deck, movement in the corner of his eye caught his attention. A man in all black came around the column closest to the car. The hair on the back of Tony's neck prickled, but he tried to ignore it. He got his keys out and put them in his good hand with keys between his fingers.

"Hola señor, necesito una palabra."

Tony stopped, then decided to throw the stranger off by not responding in the native tongue, "Are you talking to me?"

The other man's raspy English with a Nigerian accent was flawless, "Yes Antonio Garçia-Torrés, I need to speak with you about a life or death matter."

"Whose?"

"Mine and yours."

Tony was on guard more than ever, body tensing, ready to spring, "I'm listening."

The stranger stepped into the light so Tony could make him out. The man was a petite, neat black man. Though the man sported a thick beard that covered his lower face, Tony thought he might somehow know the man. "I know you have had troubles at this company recently."

"How would you know that?"

The man smirked, "Because your enemy has now become my enemy."

Tony tried to hide his genuine confusion, "I didn't know we even had an enemy. What happened between you and my supposed enemy?"

"You have a powerful faceless enemy that will do anything to get what they want, even killing people. The dock job was sloppy. Had it been done right you and I would not be talking today *señor*," the stranger smiled a crooked tooth smile. "That was definitely not my work."

Tony shot him a sour look, "So glad.

Why are you telling me this? You know the authorities are looking for you."

"They will never find me. My former employer, now that is another story." Tony finally understood but said nothing. The man continued, "Word has it that the person who did the dock job was found dead. Suicide or whatever it appeared to be."

"I thought it was an overdose," as soon as he said it, Tony realized his mistake.

The other man huffed, "There are no overdoses in my line of work. We get paid too much to be reckless. Salamanca was too smart to be reckless even though he did use. In certain circles, he was known as The Scholar, because he was smart enough to always do his research. He never took a job without making his own back door, or made insurances just in case things did not go as he planned. Someone that precise does not overdose. Look for something else in his system. I think our employer found out he was building insurances and went beyond just terminating his contract."

Tony impulsively felt sorry for the man, "I see your position. Can I help you?

"Can you help me, I think not. What they say about your family is true. Even talking to the one that tried to hurt you, still you have kind words," the black man smiled sadly. "No, I plan on disappearing but I wanted you to know the name of our enemy. That will be my insurance. All roads lead to Ares, my good man. I do not know if that is a company or a person, but I know that name was associated with the dead man."

Impulsively Tony asked, "Why us? Why this company?"

"Like I said, your family and your company have a reputation. With such a reputation, no one would question whether extra things were shipped in the cargo. The name you made remains, even if you are not the owners."

"This Ares is willing to destroy lives to try to gain access to this company because we are a solid business. Why not just pay to ship whatever they want?"

"Maybe what they want to ship is something that would be questioned if done by a lesser company," the Nigerian looked around nervously.

What the other man was eluding to finally made sense to Tony who said, "Smugglers?"

"Unheard of activity from a reputable shipping company."

"Thank you is all I can- "a car alarm went off, interrupting and startling Tony, who dropped his keys. Instinctively, he picked them up and said, "Thank you again."

But when he looked up, the stranger

was gone.

Tony's bravado was wrecked. Instead of driving home to finish his work, he walked to the closest bar for a drink. School would have to wait today.

Richard noticed his brother kept his office door closed most of the week. He knew it was nearly the end of the semester and Tony was trying to pull an exceptional grade out of his current class. Since reenrolling in college to finish his degree, Tony was putting all of his extra time and effort into being a success this time. He decided to surprise his brother with lunch. When Richard poked his head in the partially opened door of Tony's office he was confronted with a strange sight. Instead of sitting in front of the computer with a stack of books, Tony sat engrossed in thoughts so deep that he did not hear his brother. He was staring at a wall of photos of the dock, the two suspects and questions on pieces of paper beside certain pictures.

"Tony?"

He jumped as if he were poked with a pin. *"Dois mio!* Don't sneak up on me!"

Richard was truly worried, "I did not sneak up on you. The door was open and I was coming to take you to lunch. You were so deep in this . . . makeshift movie detective puzzle that you did not hear me. Tony, what is all this?"

"I'm looking for something, anything that I missed."

"What are you talking about?"

"Last week I was approached by a guy in the garage. He said he wanted to warn me about our common enemy- "

"Why didn't you tell me?" Richard exploded, "You could have been killed!"

Tony sighed in frustration at his brother's expected reaction which was why he did not tell Richard when it happened.

"Because he was not there to hurt me. Will you just listen? He let me know he wanted to talk. The guy said that Salamanca's death was not an overdose and that he was killed because he had insurance against their employer. He was going to disappear but wanted me to know the name of our common enemy was Ares. I don't know if that is a person, a company or what. He hinted to this whole mess was about using our company name for illegal activities. So, I was going over everything to see if I missed that name."

Richard was somewhere between excited with the new information and annoyed his brother kept information from him. For a moment it struck him that this must be how Mychal felt when he did the same thing to her. He put that in the back of his mind for later because right now he needed to examine this puzzle Tony was putting together so he said, "How is the end of the semester looking for you? Is that presentation on your marketing project done?"

Tony looked away, "Half done."

"*Hermano*, this is important but your classes are too. I have a great idea. Let a fresh pair of eyes look at what you have here while you go home and finish whatever you have left for class. It will give your mind a break. When you get back, you will be more focused and I will have had time to do my own work on your company mystery. *Debemos tratar*?"

Tony slowly agreed, "I guess I can agree with that. But I feel we are one missed detail away from putting everything together."

Richard put his hand on Tony's shoulder, "With the name added to the mix, I feel it too. But your professors might not feel the same. Go ahead and knock out what needs to be done. This problem will be here when you get back. I promise."

His brother put his laptop in his bag,

"That, I know to be true. If you find anything at all, call me."

"You know I will. Are you heading home or to Yadira's?"

"Home. Yadira can be distracting."

"They all are," Richard chuckled.

After finishing his immediate work, Richard returned to Tony's office with a drink and some music. It was going to be a long afternoon and possible evening. After an hour, Richard called Evan. Tony's makeshift puzzle was insightful. With the current information he was given, Tony tied all of the dock incidents to the still dead Salamanca and the garage vandalism to Demitri. The rest was connected to his mystery man with question marks.

"The kid really nailed it," Evan admired Tony's work.

"Yeah, but he has question marks just about everywhere else on this damn mystery map."

"Why is Ares a big cloud over everything?"

"Tony says his mystery man told him Ares was behind this. He is lucky he did not get killed that day."

"Like the god of war?" Evan scoffed, "Calm down. If that guy wanted Tony dead, he would never see it coming. Remember he is a professional. His job is to get things done, often times making it look like an accident and without suspicion indicating anything otherwise."

"Again, I don't think I want to know why you would know how the mind of a professional killer works. Also I have no idea whether it is like the god of war. I got *nada* which is why you are here."

"You really don't want to know," Evan shrugged. "What if that is a code or like a metaphor? Like declaring war on your company."

Richard made a skeptical face before saying, "Or a real person's name. It could be a reference to something in the Greek story of Ares. Now you understand why I have been sitting here trying to find something. Anything."

For a while the two men sat and tossed out theories. The more they drank the more far-fetched the theories got. At the end of the bottle Richard called it quits.

"I think we are going to need more people on this."

"Agreed. Let's get our computer resource involved and see if anything comes up. It maybe a few days; you know he can be ridiculously paranoid."

"That's fine. That will give my brother a few days to finish his classes. I want him in on this so he can fill in any holes from his conversation with the mystery man."

"Good plan boss man. It is the kid's

baby and maybe with his courses over, he can give this puzzle he created his full attention. I'll be in touch."

9
Mystery and Matrimony

Further investigating Tony's idea had to wait until after his sister got married and Susanna waited until after the spring semester for her nuptials. She and Mychal went dress shopping a few times. Susanna settled on a simple cream colored dress with a sweetheart neckline and wide straps. Mychal expressed the thought that the dress was a bit moderate considering what she wore as a bridesmaid in her own wedding, but Susanna explained her wedding dress for her party would be fabulous. On the last Friday of finals, a small group gathered in the garden, Tony and Yadira, Ruby and Luis, Mama Rosa and Papa Tomás Plasençia and their children that could attend, Pedro and Carmen, Uncle Rico, Mychal and Richard, and of course Carrigan.

Susanna decided against inviting her cousins, uncles and aunts to the event because she did not want to include some while exclude others, causing hurt feelings. Her ceremony was less formal than Mychal and Richard's wedding. The officiate performed the ceremony and afterward they all went to dinner. Mychal was in charge of that. She arranged for transportation to take them to a lively restaurant that had a private dining room. She made sure there would be a live band and that she could bring Carrigan's travel play pen to set up.

Getting to know Javier's family was fun. Although reserved at first, they relaxed once the food and adult beverages flowed. At one point Mychal saw Richard and Señor Plasençia singing. After the meal, the party danced to the music in the open restaurant. Mychal sat with the baby until Ruby took her and said, "Go dance with your husband. Madrina has this little girl."

Mychal went to dance with Richard who appeared to be drunk. The music was lively but Richard wanted to hold her close. She kissed him and coaxed him into dancing with her. Mychal knew Richard loved to dance and in his current frame of mind, all he needed was encouragement to really put on a show. When a slower tempo song played as Richard pulled her into his arms and sang the words to her in Castilian Spanish. Mychal knew what some of the words meant but was enthralled by the rich bass of her husband's voice. He molded his hips to hers so she could feel his desire. She blushed, which made Richard roar with laughter.

On the way back to the table he said, "*Mi Dios, tú eres tan sexy.* I think we should take a few minutes in the bathroom."

"Richard! Can you behave?"

"Oh I will Bella, but first I can imagine you with this dress pushed up and your thighs around my waist. You panting and urging me- "

"Just stop," he was turning her on, "we are around people we just met. They might hear you and think we are nymphomaniacs."

"I'm trying to be! You will not cooperate."

Mychal could not believe her ears, "You are definitely drunk."

Richard kissed her ear, "And horny. Can we call a cab to go home?"

"The car seat is in the transport van."

"Dammit woman!"

Though calmer, Richard was all hands all night. In the van he pulled her hand in his lap to stroke him. He was so hard Mychal thought the material of his pants would split. She kissed and whispered naughty things in his ear.

At home, Richard was the gracious host and saw everyone off while Mychal bathed the sleeping baby. She had just come in the room to take a shower when he came in the room, shirt already in his hand. His shoes and pants were in one pile in one move before he was on her. Fueled by desire and alcohol, Richard snatched her dress and underwear off with the speed of a superhero. He positioned them on the bed so he could please her with his mouth. She moved so they could please each other at the same time. Trying not to be distracted by her mouth and tongue, Richard's already intoxicated senses were being pushed to overload. Without warning he wrenched his hips out of her grasp, swung his body around and drove deep into her. With deliberate punctuated arching movements he drove them into bliss. Mychal held onto her husband until both their body spasms subsided. With a quick kiss Richard raised up on his knees, taking Mychal's hips with him. Pulling her legs to his shoulder, Mychal countered as Richard's pace hastened. She dug her nails into his arm until she broke skin as he thrust again and again against her round bottom. Mychal gripped his forearm tighter as his sweat dripped on her bare breast. Mychal felt her whole body explode as she exclaimed, "God I love you."

"Then give it all to me," her words stroked his passion. Even as her body trembled, Richard worked into his own frenzied release. He hugged his wife until his whole body was drained and limp. The last thing Mychal heard before drifting off was Richard's soft purr of a snore.

With their sister and new brother-in-law off to the coast of Italy for their honeymoon, the Garçia-Torrés brothers and Evan had work to do. After Evan made contact with his hacker, they added more pieces to the puzzle. Because the mystery had more levels, they moved everything to the conference room, then installed a lock.

Tony was collecting pictures to move when Morcheeba buzzed his desk, "Tony can you take a call? This guy keeps calling Richard on the private line. He will not leave a message. I have him on hold now, so will you please take the call so he will stop calling?"

"Yes, send him through." When the call connected Tony said, "Antonio Garçia-Torrés, how can I help you?"

A man with a silky smooth African accent said, "I am trying to reach Ricardo Garçia-Torrés."

"He is not available and has sent your call to me. How can I help you?"

"My name is Abiodun Otulinboson and I am calling on behalf of Demitri Salvos. It is urgent that speak with Ricardo

Garçia-Torrés immediately."

"Well sir, based on the name you just said, you will never talk with my brother," Tony just shook his head.

"Ah, you are the brother. The level headed one. My client says great things about you and how you saved her life" the smooth accent made what his short description of the actual events sound almost romantic.

"She is exaggerating, it was not all that."

"Oh yes, she speaks highly of you and is truly remorseful of how this whole unpleasant situation has affected you and your twin."

Tony was confused, so he responded 'okay' for lack of anything better to say.

"Ms. Salvos would like to apologize to your family if possible. That is why I was calling your brother. She wants to do it face to face so he can understand her sincerity."

"Again, I know my brother and the answer will be hell no." Then he added, "Sorry."

The lawyer tried again, "Perhaps you would come and speak with her? She really wants to make atonement and a brief visit from you might ease her mind."

"I am not so sure about this."

The smooth accent interrupted him, "That is not a no. Oh, thank you. I will talk with her and the prison officials today. You think about it, really think about it, and I will call you back later this week."

Before Tony could respond the call was disconnected. He stared at the phone wondering what can of snakes he had just opened. Resigned, he picked up more pictures and went down the hall to the new provisional command center. Tony plopped the pictures down on the pile. "I have come to add another piece to our puzzle."

Richard groaned loudly while Evan said, "Now what?"

"Don't act like that. As a matter of fact, you can thank my brother for this new caveat."

"What did I do?"

"You did not take the call from Abiodun Otulinboson," Tony tried his best to imitate the African accent.

"Who?" Richard was truly perplexed.

"Abiodun Otulinboson," Tony imitated the voice again, then said in his regular voice, "Demitri's lawyer."

Richard made a face at finally recognizing the name.

Evan was a little more curious, "He was trying to contact you or Richard? I am confused."

"He was trying to reach Richard. Demitri wanted to apologize in person." He went on to imitate the lawyers voice again, "She is truly remorseful of how things happened and wants to apologize in person."

"Hell no," Richard replied in a flat tone then said again, "Oh hell no!"

"I told him those exact same words."

"Great."

"But he insisted that a visit from someone would give Demitri a peace of mind."

Richard interrupted again, "Peace of mind? Who gives a damn about her peace of mind! That *novia* deserves to rot in jail for all she has done and I hope she gets traded to the other inmates for drugs every night."

Tony and Evan exchanged concerned looks.

Richard looked back at them, "Got that one from my wife. Her and her American television imagination."

Evan broke the awkward silence, "Okay *jefé*, I need you to come back from death, hell and destruction land. While I hear your very clear feelings about her, I think meeting with her might be beneficial."

Richard made another sour face and looked skeptical.

"Look, before you go off again, let's come up with a list of possible questions to ask her concerning this mess we have on our hands. She was part of it as well and maybe she can fill in some gaps," Evan tried to reason.

The room became uncomfortably quiet. After minutes of retrospect, Tony said, "Well her attorney did say she was grateful that I saved her life. I thought Mychal was going to kill her even if she said she was not. If Demitri thinks that she is indebted to me, then maybe she will want to share information with me that she might not share with you. She still might be holding on to the fantasy that she has a chance to win you back, even though you are married."

Richard's face changed slightly. Internally, he struggled with the validity of Tony's idea. On one hand they needed what she might say. On the other, he did not want to expose his family to anymore danger nor give Demitri the satisfaction of an audience. Finally, he said, "*Hermano*, I will leave that decision up to you. I have mixed emotions about this so I am no help."

Another silence engulfed the room.

Evan broke the silence again, "Regardless of your feelings, the possibility of getting additional information cannot be ignored. Tony, if you feel comfortable, then you should go. The results will outweigh the risk."

He looked at Richard who said, "If you feel comfortable is my only answer as well."

Tony sighed, "What I don't feel comfortable with is making a snap decision. Let me process this more. I will keep you posted."

The phone buzzed in the conference room and Morcheeba said, "Richard, the authorities are on line two."

Feeling like he could not catch a break today, Richard said, "Transfer them."

He put it on speaker phone, "This is Richard Garçia-Torrés."

"Señor Garçia-Torrés, this is Detective Pharr. I hate to call you but, we have a situation here at the docks. I think you should come down immediately."

"Immediately sounds serious. What is wrong now Detective?" he was really concerned and annoyed at the same time.

"Señor, there was a dead body found in a car today at your dock platform."

The three men in the room looked at each other exacerbated.

Getting to his feet, Richard said, "We will be right there detective."

After disconnecting the call all Evan could do was shake his head in disbelief. He said, "Gentleman, get ready for another piece to add to this puzzle. Or in this case, another dead body is just what we needed to add more twists to this mystery."

10
Casualties and Prisoners

Richard was over his life at the current moment. He stood outside the yellow crime scene tape looking at a man who appeared to be sleeping in his car. He knew the truth was far more gruesome. From the dashboard up was a normal man leaned back in his seat with his eyes closed, from the dashboard down was bloody to the point that it dripped out the car door. The heat did not help either. It was close to three in the afternoon, which meant the deceased exposed organs and entrails were all being baked and the bystanders overtaken by an odor that made some sick and left an impression that others would never forget. Richard was beyond thankful he skipped lunch, but his stomach still threatened to spill its liquid contents.

His workers on the other hand did not control themselves. Some gagged while others just threw up off the side of the dock. No one could leave until all names were submitted and pictures taken. The second shift was not allowed to come on premises and the work area was shut down. Not only would the day shift be paid after work was halted for the authorities, but also the second and third shifts were given the night off with pay because, again, no one could enter the crime scene. The cargo could not be unloaded, which set customs back a day and the trucking schedule had to be rerouted. On top of the notable income loss, Richard was being questioned by some crime scene investigator, who was asking for his prints.

"For what?" Richard snapped.

"To rule you out as a suspect," the guy challenged him.

"First of all, I just got here when the detective called me and second of all, my prints might be anywhere around this dock because I *am* the damn boss who comes down here sometimes daily. So no, I will *not* give you a damn thing until I speak with *your* boss. Understand?" Richard's temper was reaching the boiling point. His voice was loud and carried, making the people in the vicinity turn their heads.

"Hey, hey, I am the boss here," Detective Baird walked up behind the crime scene investigator or CSI. "You can go Parades, I will handle Señor Garçia-Torrés."

The CSI seemed grateful. When he walked away she said to Richard, "Can you give him a break today? Everybody is on edge around here. This scene was one of the worst anyone has ever seen."

Richard's temper deflated like a red balloon at a familiar face, "Sorry Baird. I guess I am just tired of whatever is going on at my company. I have never seen so many dead bodies beyond a funeral home. This incident today proved that I have seen one too many."

"As officers we get used to it, but that does not make it easy. The one thing I can tell you that from initial identification, this was our other suspect in the dock incident." She shrugged, "There is a chance that this nightmare might be over for you."

"If only I could believe that. From the looks of this scene, even I can tell he was murdered. The question now is his killer coming after me or my family?"

Detective Baird popped on blue latex gloves, "Señor, at this point, I would not go to that extreme. He was a criminal who did bad things and something terrible happened to him. Go do boss things like calming your workers far away from the crime scene. And, take the rest of your little mystery trio. You three need to leave the crime solving to the real detectives."

Richard gave her a strange face, wondering how she knew about the three of them working on putting clues together.

"I will call you if we need anything else, now goodbye," she waived him off.

He nodded goodbye and walked away wondering how that piece of information fit into his muddled mystery.

Mychal decided to take the summer semester off for research purposes. This was her second year and she had not published any articles, presented at any conferences or anything else tenure track worthy. Ruby reminded her that the first year did not count because she was a visiting professor, but Mychal felt she needed to at least start working on writing again.

First, however, she wanted to help Susanna plan her big reception, slash introduction gala. Susanna had been her right hand and left foot when it was her wedding and now she would gladly return the favor. Even as she was helping her sister-in-law, her husband was becoming increasingly distracted. When they ate dinner he was always there, but could be caught staring into space. One night she caught him off guard and asked was he happy with their marriage.

He was quite taken back, "Why would you ask? I love you and love being married to you. Why on earth would you ask that?"

"Because you are always so distracted. You are always staring into space. What is wrong? What is on your mind so heavy that you are not really here with me?"

Richard wondered if telling Mychal was a good idea. Then he remembered that day in Tony's office learning about the Nigerian. Also, since Demitri revealed her initial secret, he emphasized telling the truth in their relationship. She knew something was wrong and thought it was related to her.

With a heavy sigh, Richard laid the report he had been reading on the nightstand and told Mychal everything that happened after they found the first guy dead. He did exclude the part about their pictures on the jump drive, but let her know everything else. It felt like a boulder being lifted off his chest. He ended with his displeasure of Tony's upcoming visit with Demitri.

Mychal took in everything Richard said and noticed at the end his body got tense when he talked about his ex-girlfriend. She let him finish and asked, "What is it about the visit that you don't like?"

"How did you- " then he stopped,

realizing that he had raised his voice. "I have mixed feelings about the damn visit. On one hand, we could use any information that Tony could get. On the other hand, that *perra loca* does not deserve an audience. She deserves the next thirty years of her life in the worst prison scenario this country has to offer her."

Mychal was silent, letting him vent. She covered his hand with hers and chose her words very carefully, "She can't hurt us anymore."

"I know," his shoulders sagged, "I guess I am beyond tired. Tired of this nightmare with no end in sight. Tired of wondering if there continues to be someone out there trying to hurt my family. Tired of trying to keep my father's legacy thriving. I am . . . just . . . just . . . tired."

Mychal moved beside Richard and took him in her arms. He laid his head on her chest and relaxed. Neither said anything as they fell asleep.

Tony had only been in jail once. He was detained for questioning concerning a bar fight. He used his call to contact Uncle Rico, who immediately came and secured his release. They never told Richard. At the time, he was too drunk to notice things then, but today he was very aware and a bundle of nerves. He had to leave his keys, phone, and wallet at the check in. He was instructed not to wear shoes with laces and no jewelry. He was frisked before the gate buzzed open and he was led to a small room with a table and two chairs. Tony sat silently praying this whole situation would not blow up in his face.

The sound of chains clinking together caught his attention. The hallway was dim but Tony could make out a tall guard walking a limping hunched over old lady figure down the hall. When they stopped by the door, Tony realized the old lady figure was Demitri. He could hardly believe his eyes, in fact he blinked a few times as if the light were playing some trick on his vision. She scuffed in and quietly sat down.

Demitri looked alarming to say the least. Gone was the beauty queen of the Greek theater. Before Tony sat a broken vessel whose once glossy dark expresso colored hair looked like a silver circle around her almost unrecognizable face. The once smooth pale olive flawless complexion was now blotchy and marred with various healing scratches and bruises. The once bright brown eyes were dull as cold black coffee with enough bags under them to rival a commercial airline flight. The graceful model walk was now a limp made more pronounced by the restrictive chains. Tony was mesmerized by the change since he had last seen her cowering for her life. His stare was broken by Demitri saying, "Thank you for coming. I knew your brother would say no, but you would be as kind to me as you always were."

He found his voice, "Well, your lawyer was insistent."

She smiled, "He does his job. How is Richard?"

"He's good," Tony gave her a simple answer.

"I am glad to hear that." Demitri paused, "I wanted to apologize to you about the car incident. I really was not trying to hurt you.

"I know but," he stumbled looking for the right words, "you did hurt me and those incidents at the docks almost killed me, Richard and more than a hundred people. Pardon my honesty, but I am struggling with your apology"

Demitri looked hurt at his words, "I am sincere. I realized I was so wrong to hurt you and my dear Richard. But I never wanted you dead. The incident at the docks was not me. Though I found out about it later, I had nothing to do with it."

"But, why didn't you tell someone? Especially if you knew who did it?"

"Tony, I found out later as in months later from chance encounter with Rafael's family. By then everything was over and I was so mad with your brother that all I wanted was to hurt him," she shrugged.

"If we had known any information we could have put in safety measures- "

Demitri interrupted, "You hired enough security for a personal army!"

"We could have saved their lives!" Tony almost shouted. "Both men that were involved are dead and we are no closer to finding out who hired them."

She turned as white as fresh snow, "Both men are dead? The addict and the Nigerian?"

"You knew? How did you know? You are in prison!" Tony was surprised.

"My lawyer told me about the addict, Salamanca. He told me that after the guy was found there was evidence that proved that I was no longer a suspect related to the matter. Then he told me the authorities were still looking for the Nigerian mercenary as a suspect in the dock incident," she seemed distracted and far away.

"The Nigerian said the dock job was sloppy and he had nothing to do with it," Tony blurted out then felt stupid for sharing too much information.

Demitri gave him a suspicious look, "You actually talked to him? Where did you talk with the Nigerian mercenary and lived to tell? What did he say?"

Cautious he replied, "He came to me at work in the parking garage. He said he was not there to hurt me, just talk. He said the dock incident was not his work. He told me to be careful of some company and its owner."

Tony paused, then decided to go on a fishing expedition, "I think he mentioned some Greek name. Zeus, Apollo, or something."

"Ares," she whispered.

"I think that is what he said. How did you know?"

Demitri did not reply.

Tony leaned in, "Demitri how do you know that name?"

"You have never heard of that company?"

"Should I?"

She looked nervous, "I guess you would not. Ares is a major political player in Greece. When the economy crashed a few years back, a few companies including

Ares stepped in to offer support to the government during that time."

Tony was more confused than ever, "Why would some foreign company be involved in trying to sabotage my family's company? We are not some global players that regularly attend the G20 summit."

Demitri sadly smiled at his comment, "I have no answers for you."

"Well, what can you tell me?"

"That I have said too much and you should be thankful that you are alive today. My final advice is that this whole ordeal is not over."

"How can you say that? The saboteurs are dead," Tony tried not to show his new frustration at her comment.

"Their deaths are probably part of a clean-up effort. Ares has been rumored for years to have ties with globalized organized crime," Demitri suddenly looked defeated.

The light dimmed in her eyes and worry lines appeared across her forehead. "Heaven help me."

"Why do you say that?"

She rose, kissed her fingers and placed them on his hand. She tapped the bars for the guard, "Because again, I have said too much. If you want to know more, you should ask your neighbor."

More exacerbated than ever Tony asked, "The only neighbor I talk to is Rafael. Why would I need to talk to him?"

As she scuffed out the door Demitri looked back and replied quietly, "Because the founder of Ares, Delossantos, is Rafael's uncle."

When Tony relayed his conversation with Demitri to Evan and Richard, the room was silent. The three men had sporadic conversation over the next hour, not really knowing what to say. Toward the end, the group had to call in the computer consultant whose first order of business was to provide them with the correct name: Amato Delossantos. Even with the new information, each man left their provisional command center with a different reaction. Evan was excited, Tony was confused and Richard was preoccupied with mixed emotions. He was angry and depressed, sullen and focused, anxious and apprehensive.

At home his mood did not improve. He interacted with Mychal and the baby, but it was not as engaged as usual. Richard asked Mychal to put Carrigan to bed for him before slipping into his office. Once there he searched for any clue the internet might offer to give him insight into his growing problem. He was so focused that he did not hear his wife come in. When she touched his shoulders, he almost jumped out of his skin. *"Dios mío, no me asusta!"*

Mychal did not say a word at first. She gave Richard a tolerating look and then said in her best silly southern grandmother voice, "Let's start over. Hi honey. Are you okay? You were so distracted at dinner. Is there anything I can do to help you, you poor thing you?"

Richard blinked at her silliness.

She patted his hand, "You looked tired and overworked. Bless your heart."

He tried to take her seriously but the awful southern drawl got him. Finally, he shook his head and smiled, "There is nothing sexy about your grandmother voice. That is the worst impression of a southern grandmother in the history of the world."

Mychal continued, "Child, how do you know? You don't even know any people from the south. And going to school in Florida does not count."

"What? Yes it does."

She patted his hand again, "It's okay not to have any southern friends. Bless your little heart."

Richard captured her hand and pulled her into his lap. Once there, he gave his wife a deep and passionate kiss. She responded, feeling the heat from his mouth start to spread. This was not why Mychal came to his office. She broke their kiss and Richard immediately started on her neck. "Honey, what's wrong?"

"Nothing now."

In a sterner voice she said, "I'm serious. I came in here to check on you. All night your body has been with us but your mind is God knows where. What's bothering you?"

Richard hugged Mychal and buried his face in her hair, "Do I have to?"

"You do. If I have to suffer, at least let me know why."

After a long sigh, he told her about Tony's visit with Demitri. Mychal already

241

knew he was upset before the visit so his reaction now made more sense. He did not tell her everything but concluded with they were trying to figure out why and what some company based in Greece wanted with his shipping business, especially a corporation like Ares which was mostly into various financial avenues. He left out the one clue of the name they already had that was given to Tony.

"Richard perhaps you need to think outside the box on this one."

He gave Mychal a 'where are you going with this' look.

She smiled back, "I need you to think beyond the 'ruin my company' premise. Ask yourself, is this a personal matter? Is it tied to your family's history in any way? Are there any legal issues, past or present? Any near future legislation that will affect the shipping business? There is a reason the other company went to such extremes that people lost and almost lost their lives. Whatever the reason, it has meaning to that company, either trivial or on some larger scale."

When he did not respond, she kissed him on the lips, *"Buena noche guapo."*

"You are just going to leave me?"

"Oh yeah, because you have work to do. You need to get a handle on this and the emotional ball of nerves you are now. Me and Carrigan need you and this situation is changing you. So fix it. The sooner this is over, the sooner I get the man I married back."

"You know I love you."

"I know and I love you too. Now get to work." She paused at the door, "I almost forgot why I even came in here."

"I thought it was to tease me with that perfect round behind and those perky peach-"

Mychal blushed at Richard's boldness, "Will you stop flirting, you dirty old man? I came to tell you that I talked with Riley a few minutes ago. Jacob's lawyer thinks they have worked out a plea deal. There is light on the horizon."

11
Scandals and Fiestas

Richard and Mychal's one year anniversary was ushered in by a sick teething baby. Mychal had never seen Carrigan so cranky. Her godparents came over so Luis could check her out. He took her downstairs to the library where Richard kept a stocked bar. Luis put a little liquor on his finger and rubbed her gums. The new sensation was strange to the infant who mashed her godfather's pinky between the gums on her left side. Luis had Mychal search the internet for local pharmacies that sold chamomile tablets, then sent her and

Ruby to get some along with a small list of items that would help the infant.

While the wives were gone, Luis and Richard discussed upcoming plans. Luis told Richard his plans to buy a boat and a small flat in the Mediterranean country side. Richard shared the latest work issues including Tony's visit with Demitri. He talked openly to Luis about his feelings for Demitri and the fact that in his mind, she was dead to him.

"That was harsh," Luis interjected.

"I know, but the more I think about her trying to kill my wife and child, I get angry all over again."

The older man shook his head, "Your hatred toward her is affecting you. Listen to yourself and look at your body language. You have to let that go."

Richard frowned, "You are asking

for the impossible. I will never forgive her."

"Forgive her or forgive you?"

"What?"

"Nelson Mandela once said not forgiving someone is like drinking poison and expecting the other person to die. You heard what I said. Are you holding resentment because you cannot forgive her for what she almost did to your family or forgive yourself for letting your guard down when it came to your old friend?"

Richard's expression softened as the words hit their intended mark of the truth, but he said nothing.

"Do you see this precious angel in my arms?" Luis motioned to Carrigan, "She is the reason you must do both. All the energy you use holding a grudge could be energy put in more positive things like work or your family. You decide. But holding on to those negative thoughts and emotions will become a lasting barrier to being the best you. Someone I call my friend."

Richard was quiet. Luis' words struck a chord. He looked at the face of his sleeping daughter, making the decision to follow his friend's advice. He smiled at Luis, who read his mind and said, *"Buena elección señor."*

Mychal took a week off from researching her book for two reasons, one to help Susanna with her gala and two to celebrate Richard's birthday.

A few days before his birthday she left a black velvet box on the night stand. The next day his favorite bottle of scotch was on his desk at work with a bow. The day before his birthday a courier delivered a box with new cuff links attached to only the cuff part of a shirt. The note read 'appropriate dress for tomorrow night'.

Richard was both intrigued and excited about having no idea what his wife was planning.

On his actual birthday they made love in the morning then had breakfast in bed with their daughter. Richard's mind was distracted at work wondering what kind of dinner plans included just cuffs and links. Evan, Morcheeba, and Tony took him out for a lunch siesta to make sure his birthday was spent away from the problems at work.

After putting the baby to bad, Richard met Mychal downstairs for a late dinner in cuff, links and his necklace. He was treated to a three course meal with fruits and cream for dessert. Mychal served him in a straps and lace French maid outfit with fishnets and stilettos. As she brought out his dishes, she made sure to brush different parts of his body. During dessert in front of the fireplace, he continued to enjoy his wife's seductions. Under the light of the fire, they made love until after midnight.

With Richard in a good mood following his birthday, it was time to focus on the upcoming gala. While Susanna worked on the items for her silent auction, Mychal coordinated food. She technically cheated because she used the same caterer from her wedding. Mychal changed some of the menu items and advised Javier to order whatever wine he wanted from Papa Plasençia's shop. He told her his adopted father would not take any payment, so he was donating the wines as a gift to his son and his new wife.

Since Mychal had no idea what gala decorations should look like, she spent days on the internet trying to find ideas and themes. She finally came up with an idea that would incorporate the company's mission with the decorations and colors. It took more days to coordinate the idea, but Mychal pulled everything together while keeping it a secret.

The next step was finding a dress that would be appropriate to double for a wedding dress as well as a charity event dress. This task was slightly more difficult with an infant. Mychal made sure she had everything Carrigan needed, especially teething medication. After a week they found a dress that Susanna had her heart set on. Mychal bought it as a belated wedding present. As Susanna was talking about alterations with the seamstress, Mychal took pictures of the baby with a tiny tiara on her head and sent it to Richard with the message 'Someday'. He sent back a string of emojis including a frowning one, crying one and a foul language one. She had to laugh because it was clear her husband had no idea how to correctly use emojis or he was feeling some kind of way.

The night of the gala Carrigan was on her way to Abeulita Carmen's house while her parents got dressed. Mychal dropped the baby off and stopped by Susanna's place to get her make up done.

She came in the suite and could tell Richard's great mood, which was evident as he hummed while he shaved.

She poked her head in, "Where's your stuff?"

"On the back of the closet door. You look gorgeous," he winked.

"You are just saying that so I will give you something other than a good night kiss."

Richard's smiled broadened, "Yes, yes I am."

But his wife really did look good. Her original shape was back with a little thickness plus she added tone arms. Iroh deserved a bonus for a wife this good looking.

"Are you going to take much longer?"

He splashed aftershave on, "Nobody

did my makeup."

"I even took the baby across the property. What are you doing that is taking so long?"

Ignoring his wife, Richard went to the closet to get his freshly cleaned tux. "I was a little distracted earlier. I stayed in the shower thinking about my parents for a minute."

Mychal knew this night all three siblings had similar thoughts and emotions. Susanna said so in the apartment and Yadira commented that Tony shared his feelings about missing their parents that morning. She stepped into her gold one shoulder gown. Mychal pulled out the velvet box containing her emerald and gold jewelry while waiting for Richard to zip her up. After a few moments she called, "What are you doing?"

"Come help me."

Mychal became alarmed. She rushed

to the closet to see Richard standing with a wide grin on his face.

"What in the hell? I thought something was wrong."

"I said come help me . . . celebrate our anniversary," he opened a black velvet box that held a pendant and matching earrings. The pendant itself was the size of a business card with the center diamond surrounded by smaller blue diamonds. The earrings were a quarter of the size of the matching pendant.

"Oh my God Richard! Honey, they are stunning."

He mentally patted himself on the back, "Let me put them on."

Mychal turned so he could put on the necklace and zip her dress. Richard whispered in her ear, "Thank you for being my wife."

She turned and kissed him

passionately. Richard returned her kiss until he felt the beginnings of a familiar rigidness. He broke the kiss, "We need to get this event started. The sooner we get this over with the sooner I can see you in nothing but diamonds."

Mychal blushed, "You bet, daddy."

Richard grinned, "I like the sound of that."

Once again the front lawn was transformed into a place for an elegant affair. Security was in place as usual, checking people in a small white tent adjacent to the valet stand as they dropped off cars to the valet. Mychal and Richard entered from the back as the pool house was set up for restrooms. Mychal was anxious to see how her decoration ideas looked. She had the pictures, but wanted to see how everything turned out once the lights and colors were added to the centerpieces.

People kept stopping Richard, so she sent him away to be the proud patriarch with a kiss.

Walking around, Mychal was electrified with excitement. The first table she came to was a trumpet with small peach flowers and tiny LED lights intertwined around the mouth piece and keys. The next table contained a clarinet with a different blue flower and the same tiny LED lights. Mychal smiled at how her smart little idea worked out. Her thoughts were interrupted by a guest that recognized her, but she was not sure how she knew the woman. After a few minutes of polite conversation, Mychal saw an escape in Uncle Juan.

She excused herself and made a beeline to him. From Uncle Juan, Mychal bounced from conversation to conversation with people she was familiar with. She was talking with Morcheeba about dating when Susanna found her.

"Mychal, these decorations are gorgeous. What a creative idea," Susanna was glowing in her after ceremony dress. The top was an antique strapless white bodice adorned in pearls and crystals that flowed into a satin skirt. Mychal could see Susanna's French pedicure poking out.

"You are absolutely beautiful tonight. That dress is much daintier than I thought. And I love the hair down."

Susanna blushed.

"Where is your husband? Does he know you left his side?" Morcheeba joked.

"He is trying to hide. This is definitely not his comfort zone."

Mychal could only imagine Javier's anxiety level. She was broken out of her thoughts by Susanna saying, "Come on Mychal, it is time for the show."

The event hostess was motioning for them to hurry. She flipped Mychal the microphone and mouthed "in English".

"Ladies and gentlemen," she heard Uncle Rico translate, "Welcome to the annual charity event for Transition Notes, where we foster healing through music. If you will please take a seat, the program introduction will begin."

The audience moved around to find a seat as the eight-foot screen lit up with a short film showcasing the goals and purpose of Susanna's company. Mychal could see she put a lot of work into the video. It displayed Susanna working with children and adults, included biographical information of various famous celebrity musicians that were born with disabilities. The video closed with ways contributions would help the organization. As the music died Susanna came on stage with a microphone.

First, she thanked the audience for coming. Next, she talked about the foundation's goals and objectives over the next five years. Susanna then wanted to thank her support team. She called her husband Javier on stage. He emerged from the crowd looking unnerved. As Javier walked onto the platform, Susanna told the audience how he was her rock that anchored her through the entire process and without his love and support, her dream would have never become reality. When he got on the stage she hugged and kissed him. The audience applauded.

Susanna called Tony on stage. As he walked up she spoke about how having her brother as a twin motivated her to start the organization and how his fresh ideas were vital in the developmental stages of the foundation. When Tony hugged his sister, there was more applause.

Next, she called Richard to the stage. He gave Mychal a look, but she shooed him to go up. Susanna got emotional as she discussed how her oldest brother stepped up to guide her as their father would have. She told how after making sure she had a sound business plan, he gave all the support she needed including the party. Susanna ended with how much the love of her older brother fostered her love to help others, just as Rohas and Alejandra Garçia-Torrés would have wanted.. When Richard hugged and kissed Susanna, she wiped tears. The audience erupted in applause with people rising to their feet.

She took a breath and thanked Uncle Rico and Mychal. Richard urged them both on stage. She thanked Uncle Rico for his legal guidance and Mychal for basically planning the event along with the beautiful decorations. Uncle Rico blew Susanna a kiss and Mychal mouthed, 'The instruments are yours'. Richard motioned to the microphone still in her hand.

Mychal said, "The instruments that decorate the table will be donated to the foundation after the event."

Susanna squealed like a school girl. She leaned in front of Richard to squeeze

Mychal's hand. In closing Susanna said, "Please participate in the auction. Thank you all for coming out and your support. And finally enjoy your evening. *Beber, bailar y festejar!*"

The audience stood on their feet again applauding as everyone left the platform stage. Mychal was glad that was over so she could enjoy time with her husband. But first she wanted to check on Javier who looked as anxious as an injured dolphin in a shark tank.

As Mychal approached Javier and Susanna, she noticed a tall, thin but dignified gentleman had them captured in conversation. She saw Javier's whole body stiffen and his face darken. She walked up to hear a bit of the discussion.

"It is such a pleasure to meet you. I had no idea my son was married," the older gentleman said.

Susanna politely replied, "We chose

to tell the people that mattered the most about our wedding."

"How did you even get invited to this?" Javier interjected.

"It is a fundraiser for the arts. How could I miss this, especially since the invitation came from the Garçia-Torrés family?" The man calling Javier his son smiled, "Imagine my surprise seeing my son all grown up and married to the only daughter of Rohas Garçia-Torrés. Congratulations my son, you have done well for yourself."

"No thanks to you," Javier snapped back.

Mychal knew it was time to intervene, "Oh there you two are! I have been looking everywhere for you."

All eyes turned to her.

"There is someone here from a British magazine that needs a picture of you two to go with the review of this event." She turned to the tall gentleman and sweetly said, "You don't mind if I borrow them for just a minute, do you?"

"Anything for Ricardo's beautiful American wife," he purred, almost flirting.

"Why, thank you on both accounts. I knew a wonderful gentleman such as yourself would more than understand," she poured on the charm. "Come on you two, she's right near the auction table."

Mychal swiped Susanna's hand and pulled her away with Javier following. They were barely out of earshot when she said, "You can thank me later for that."

Javier was surprised, "How did you know?"

"Your whole attitude."

"So where is the magazine person?" Susanna asked.

"There was no magazine person. I just saw your husband looking like he wanted to fight and I lied to get you away."

"*Gracias*," Javier relaxed and smiled.

"*Su nada*, now go enjoy your night and avoid Mr. I Am So Important."

Susanna sighed, "I could spend the rest of my life avoiding my would be pious father-in-law."

Mychal noted the comment but said, "Well go. This is your night."

When she finally caught up with Richard he hugged and kissed her passionately. He whispered in her ear, "I wanted to do that all night."

"I missed you too. Have you been playing your favorite roll of gracious host, this time soliciting donations for your sister?"

"Have I ever? I have shaken so

many hands that I need a bath right now. Want to join me in a few?"

Mychal smiled at her husband's suggestion, "Later for sure. Right now, I'm going to stay close to the newlyweds. I thought something was wrong with Javier on stage earlier and I was right."

Richard commented, "He was acting kind of wooden."

"I know. So afterward I wanted to check on him and some older guy had them locked in some awkward conversation. So I rescued them by lying about a photograph. When I got them away, Susanna said that man was Javier's father. He was acting like an ass, praising Javier for marrying Susanna like he bought a prize winning racehorse or something," Mychal tried to control her disdain.

"Señor Plasençia was not around was he?" Richard asked.

"No. Why?"

"Señor Plasençia hates Javier's father and although he is a little old man, believe me when I tell you that he would let his temper get the best of him; especially on this special occasion."

Mychal smiled a little at the protectiveness she heard in Richard's voice. "This man was super tall, thin as a rail with a mess of snow white hair. It was combed over to cover the beginnings of a bald spot. He even mentioned your father's name and commended Javier for marrying a Garçia-Torrés. Pompous ass."

Richard was frowning, but said, "You said super tall. Like over six feet tall?"

"More like six eight. He could have been a basketball player back in his day."

"He was," Richard replied, "now he is a deputy of congress. You are right, he is a pompous jerk. My father dealt with him in local politics. I, unfortunately, have to deal with Señor Aranejui de Taveras in occasional business dealings. If I had known he was Javier's real father, after everything Susanna has told me, I would have never invited him."

"But you didn't know, and for all intense purposes Señor Plasençia is who I consider Javier's father." Mychal took his hand and squeezed it, "Javier and I have a little something in common."

"I know," Richard kissed her forehead, "and that is why this situation bothers you."

She smiled, "A little, but Javier is a survivor. He is going places and I hate the wolves in this world see his destiny as a way for them to get an inside angle."

"True." Richard switched subjects, "Can you do me a favor and check on the Plasençia family? I need to collaborate with Uncle Rico concerning one unique donation. Once I finish with him, I will come find you. Okay?"

"No problem sexy," Mychal blew him a kiss.

No sooner than Mychal was out of sight, Richard went to find Tony, Uncle Juan and Uncle Rico. He needed to set things straight with the local deputy of congress once and for all.

The impromptu meeting of the five men was held in the library. Richard needed Tony, Uncle Rico and Uncle Juan there for diplomacy sake because he had no intentions of civility. However, his uncles took over the meeting. Uncle Juan recalled the scandalous affair that produced Javier, while Uncle Rico talked about how Señor Aranejui de Taveras' lost face in the community and almost lost his position. Richard and Tony gave each other the what-in-the-hell-is-going-on-here look. While Uncle Juan reminded the deputy of his other little known affairs that his wife would not want to hear, Uncle Rico added such behavior if publicly known could ruin such a longstanding political career.

The tense silence was thick in the room until the deputy asked were they done.

Richard spoke up by warning the important official to stay away from his sister and her husband, then asked him politely to leave. He finished by saying the meeting never happened. Richard put his ear piece in and told security to notify him when the deputy of congress left the premises. With that bit of business done, he went to find his wife to enjoy the rest of the evening.

After seeking out the Plasençias to exchange pleasantries about Javier and Susanna, Richard found Mychal hanging out with Luis and Ruby. He greeted them and had small talk for a few minutes before sweeping his wife on the dance floor. They moved like magic to a few songs before needing a cool drink.

As the night wore on, Ruby and Luis, along with several guests filtered out. Mychal and Richard sat drinking and talking with Evan and his date Detective Felecity "Lee" Baird. Mychal had never seen Evan look so nice. He looked like a different person in his tailored tux. His sun bleached caramel colored hair that was always barely managed in a ponytail was neatly groomed and hung on his shoulders. His date wore a black floor length Queen Anne neckline dress with plain gold accessories. His slender surfer frame complimented her matching willowy frame nicely. Their conversation was interrupted by a call on her work phone. She was gone so long on the call that Evan went to find her. He came back and said he needed to speak with Richard about a security matter. When they got to the security booth, Detective Baird was collecting her coat.

"Is something wrong? Why are you leaving?" Richard was concerned.

The detective shot Evan an uneasy

look. He turned to Richard and said, "She has to go to work. There might be a homicide in connection with the other murders in the case they have been working on."

"As in our case?"

"Yes." Then she sighed, "Señor Garçia-Torrés, Richard, I cannot tell you anything due to complications. I am sure you understand."

"Complications?" Richard's patience slipped a little, "Come on Baird, stop being so damn secretive and tell me what the hell is going on."

"We have to tell him babe. No, I have to tell him. He is more than my boss, he is my friend."

The detective sighed and nodded okay before the car pulled up.

"Evan, what's going on?"

Evan put a hand on Richard's shoulder, "Sorry to tell you this, Demitri was found dead in her cell tonight. The authorities are not sure if she hung herself or if it was staged to look that way."

Richard was stunned beyond silent.

"I'll be in touch when I know something." Evan got in the car, *"Lo siento jefé."*

12
Repercussions and Relations

Richard sat on the information about Demitri's death for twenty-four hours. He did not want it to ruin the rest of the evening. So after closing out the event and making passionate love to his wife in the twilight hours of the morning, he told her over a late breakfast the next day.

"Why are you just telling me now if this happened yesterday?" Mychal was a little taken by surprise.

"I guess I needed time to process everything."

Mychal gave Carrigan a piece of banana, "You okay?"

Richard shrugged, "I guess I do not really know what I feel. I mean, I feel like I am mourning the passing of a forgotten friend but I am relieved that such a hateful person cannot harm anybody else. I have never had a person I despise die."

Mychal thought about that for a moment, then said, "I guess that is how I am feeling right now too. I wanted her to suffer, not die."

"Exactly."

"Now, I'm questioning whether it was wrong to want her to suffer."

Richard nodded in agreement.

"Well, let's change the subject. I think Ma is coming for the christening," Mychal made a funny face.

Richard was glad to switch subjects,

especially to one he was excited about. While they talked about having family at the house again, he decided to call Max after visiting his siblings. The visit to their apartment went as Richard thought it would. Susanna was saddened and Tony was quiet upon hearing the news. He asked Richard was he the last person to see her alive. With questions like that, Richard knew his brother needed time to process what he just heard and he would check with him later that night.

After lunch the following Monday, Detectives Baird and Pharr paid Richard a visit.

"Detectives, good to see you, though I cannot say it is a surprise," he sat back in his chair.

"No Señor Garçia-Torrés it is not a surprise and is an official business call," Detective Baird spoke up.

"Really?"

"Ms. Salvos was found dead over the weekend in her cell."

Richard sighed, "I know."

"There is an investigation because her cause of death has yet to be determined. I just needed to ask a few questions to help us out here. Can you think of anybody that would want Ms. Salvos dead?"

"Just a few to my knowledge, my neighbor Rafael and I guess my wife. But I would really exclude her because she had the chance to hurt Demitri but refrained."

"Yes, I remember," Detective Pharr nodded. "When we arrived at the scene Ms. Salvos was in bad shape."

Richard gave a calculated response, "You should remember that she was trying to kill my wife and Mychal defended herself. I think the pregnancy hormones and adrenaline took over. The possibility of my wife and daughter being killed is a terrible thought that still haunts me."

"That is understandable señor," Detective Baird said softly. Then she asked, "As a point of protocol, where was your wife Saturday night?"

"At my sister's charity event. She even did some ceremonial duties around the main presentation."

"And your neighbor? Was he there?"

Richard thought for a minute, just realizing that although he was invited, Rafael was not in attendance. He frowned and replied, "I honestly do not remember seeing him there. I know we invited him as we always do, but I did not see him that night. He does not get out much since Demitri's attack. He is dealing with a lot of physical and mental scarring."

"Do you interact with your neighbor much?" the other man asked.

"No more than before. He is closer in age to my siblings. I am his neighbor, not a close friend."

"One last question, you said Señor Decarvalho was physically scarred and does not get out much. Do you know this because you have seen him recently?" Detective Baird was fishing.

"I saw him once after his attack. He had a walking cane, could barely get out of a chair and his sister had moved in to assist with his care. If you think he is a questionable suspect when it comes to her, my answer is this: we would all like to see the person that harmed us receive their due justice. He is only a human, who almost died at the hands of a woman he thought loved him. That would make half the planet quote unquote questionable."

"*Gracias señor*. We will be in touch with any more questions." The detectives left feeling as though Richard was no help and had no intention of helping.

After work, Richard impulsively

decided to visit Rafael. He was both glad and shocked when he answered the door.

"Richard, es bueno ver que el viejo. What do I owe the honor of this visit?"

Richard shook his hand that was not used to support his cane. "I needed to talk with you about something I thought you should know."

"Come in," his neighbor led him into the spacious den with the panoramic view. "Drink?"

Richard declined and when Rafael sat down, he told him Demitri was dead. Rafael was full of questions. What happened? When did she die? Richard told him what the detectives relayed which was a suspicious death with the possibility of suicide. Then he told his neighbor about the police coming to his office with questions about people who would want her dead. He finally told Rafael the police might question him too.

"Why?"

Richard eyed Rafael for a reaction as he said, "Because they think you might have a reason to want her dead."

"Death would have been too easy," Rafael replied bitterly. "She needed to suffer, the way I suffer every day. She needed to rot in a prison cell every day until she expired, natural or otherwise."

Richard was apathetic at the other men's response. He had feelings along those same lines. He let Rafael vent a bit before saying, "Of all people, I truly understand."

A silence hung between them.

Richard had two reasons for coming to see his neighbor. One was to honestly tell Rafael the truth. The other was to do a little research of his own. He needed to know was his neighbor connected to the murders in any way. He also needed to know was Rafael a threat to his family.

Carefully Richard crafted his next words. He needed his lie to sound convincing enough to make the other man let his guard down. "When the police came to talk with me, they said Demitri was telling the guards Amato Delossantos was going to make her pay for hurting his nephew. I told them I did not know who that person was other than them telling me he was your uncle."

"Uncle Mato?" Rafael was skeptical, "He's my mother's oldest brother, well half-brother. He's like the most docile eighty year old man in the world. I think he and Demitri met one time. They are both from Greece and shared a conversation about the theatre, naturally. Why would she say something so outrageous?"

"I have no idea, but the police might ask you about that. Thought you might want the heads up," he rose to leave.

"Thanks for the information."

"No problem. It was good to see you. You look better, more like your playboy self," Richard joked.

"Ah, it takes one to know one," Rafael laughed, "but now you are retired."

Richard chuckled, "Yes, I am and one day you will be too."

"One day."

As he exited the room, Rafael said, "As cold as it sounds, justice was served. She got what she deserved."

Richard kept walking like he did not hear a word. His mind was already processing the new information and how it fit into the whole twisted situation.

Even though Max would be at the house in a few days, Richard needed to talk with him, without Mychal. So he stayed at work one evening to call him.

"Richard, what's going on?"

He sat back in his chair and loosened up his tie, "More of the same. And you?"

"Getting ready to take that flight in two days. Is anything wrong?"

"No, just needed to have a private word with just you. How's the case going? Has there been any news?"

Max sighed, "It is hard to tell. Riley is depressed and isolates herself from everybody. When I call her, she seems spacey and will not talk about Jacob. I thought him even considering a plea deal would make this better."

"Mychal says the same. When they talk on the phone, Riley rarely wants to talk to her and always wants to talk to the baby," Richard recalled. "I wish she was coming. Maybe we could talk some sense into her."

"You offered Richard, but I knew she was not coming. I see that same old jealousy resurfacing in her life and hear it in her slick comments. I know they are sisters but it seems the more they make progress, the more they regress. For all intents and purposes, I think it was best she sits this one out."

"If you say so. Regardless, I love seeing the family."

"Yeah, Gwen is so excited. She says we never get a vacation. Reese and Yvonne are thrilled too. I have talked to my brother almost daily about what to expect. He hopes the two of you will get along."

Richard scoffed, "He's great. My wife clearly shows favoritism, but loves her siblings just the same. I am looking forward to meeting my other family members in person."

Richard actually was eager to meet Reese. Like he told Max, Mychal's favorite was him, but she equally loved and talked to Reese. He seemed to have that same easy demeanor as his older brother, but was a bit more vocal with less tact about speaking his mind. He talked a little more with Max before hanging up to focus on a brewing idea.

Mychal, Carrigan and Iroh were waiting for her family at the airport. She saw Gwen first and burst into smiles.

"Girl, you look great," her sister-in-law hugged her.

Mychal hugged back, "I'm so glad you could come. Are the kids okay now? I know they wanted to come."

"They are going to be okay. Busy sulking because they claim it wasn't fair they had to stay home. But Zander had tryouts and stayed with friends. Xavier wanted to hang with your mother. She spoils him so terrible," Gwen shook her head.

"Hey, don't hog my sister," Reese walked up. Mychal hugged her baby brother tightly. She was almost in tears that he actually came to visit. When he saw this he said, "Oh, come on ya damn softy, kill the waterworks."

"Reese, I'm just so happy . . . " she trailed off.

He hugged her again, "I know sis, and it has been too long."

Max and Reese's wife Yvonne walked up. Mychal smiled while wiping tears.

"There you are," Max hugged his sister.

"Hello Doc," Yvonne waited for her hug. Reese's wife was always soft spoken. She had a curt North Florida accent. Yvonne, who was three inches taller than her husband, had the most distinguishing features. Her skin was the color of Frappuccino covered in coffee colored freckles. Mychal often wondered if her appearance was the reason she was so quiet. She had a son from a previous marriage and they had a girl.

"How are my niece and nephew?"

"Sour because we went somewhere without them and they are home with Riley."

"How do you think Riley is really doing?"

Yvonne rolled her eyes, "What I think she is doing . . . is the most right now. She calls Reese whenever to just cry. You know he has been very supportive, but the calls cut into his sleep time during the work week. And she knows that! I wish that punk ass husband would just take the damn deal so this whole mess could be over."

"You know I know," Mychal shook

her head, "but for now, leave that worry home and let's enjoy ourselves."

Everyone was crowded around Max, who was holding Carrigan.

"Where's Iroh?"

"Your funny assistant," Reese replied, "went to get the car. Let's get our bags and get this show on the road."

Her brothers retrieved the luggage while Mychal and her sisters-in-law went to wait for Iroh on the curve. The ride to the house was filled with questions about the scenery.

Reese leaned over and said, "Max told me that guy is your babysitter too. What the hell sis?"

"He's family as far as we are concerned," Mychal answered. She did not know how much information her mother and Max told Reese.

He shot her a cynical look. He gave her another crazy look as they passed the temporary guard station. Richard's new Aston Martin Sedan was parked in the circular driveway. Mychal knew he was excited to see Max and hoped that excitement would extend to Reese. As soon as the car stopped, Richard came out the front door wearing brown leather sandals, wheat linen slacks and a deep purple polo shirt. God, he looked so sexy to Mychal.

Her sisters-in-law must have thought so as well. Yvonne made the comment 'Oh girl' while Gwen said 'Um uh'.

"Max!" Richard hugged one of his favorite people as soon as he got out of the truck. "Good to see you."

When Reese got out of the truck, he hugged him as well. Reese had his hand out at first, but Richard said, "We're family, we hug."

The women got out and Iroh got the bags to put in the house. Richard addressed each wife by name and hugged them. He took the carrier from Mychal and kissed her. She whispered something in his ear and he kissed her again. Richard ushered them in the house.

While Mychal changed the baby, Richard walked them around the property and introduced their scent to the dogs. When he came back to take them upstairs to their rooms, Solomon came to check out Mychal. With the baby napping in the play pen, she went outside to play with him. Richard came out a few minutes later asking, "Is Susanna home?"

"Probably not. She said she would see us tonight if she could. I think she is looking for a building."

"She did mention they were doing that today. Well, I have something in the pool house to show you."

Mychal gave him a look, "What did you buy for the baby?"

Richard reached in his pocket and threw the dog a treat, "Just come see."

They walked to the pool house and once inside she scanned the room for a new baby toy or slide, which Richard mentioned weeks earlier. Instead he kissed her ear while pulling her bottom against his rigidness. She smiled at his slyness, enjoying his body movements that stirred her core.

"Honey, we have guest. There is no time for that."

She felt him again pressed against her bottom, this time the material barrier was gone. He whispered in her ear a reminder of her earlier statement, "There is always time to let you know there is more to me than just sexy as hell."

She turned in his arms, pulling him to meet her hungry mouth. As if he was in some invisible race, Richard had them on the settee, her underwear gone, and joined in demanding desire. His pace meant business from the start as his movements quickly worked them toward a blissful release. They spent a few moments holding each other before Richard joked that she should not trick him into the pool house again while they had guests. For that she popped him on the butt while they recovered clothing. They walked back to the house, each glowing with a secret smile.

For dinner, the three couples went out. They met Luis and Ruby at a local restaurant and went for tapas and dancing afterward. As the others danced Reese slid next to his sister, "So are you having fun?"

"Oh yeah. Are you?"

He gave her a broad grin, "You bet. Richard is like another brother. I still can't believe this guy thought you were a dude when he hired you."

"Strange beginnings right?"

"You know when Riley came back from the wedding she was different. She was a cross between resigned and angry, making her way oversensitive. Max said you two got into it."

Mychal sighed, "We passed new words on the same old subject. Same Riley same- "

He interrupted, "Let me guess the 'mom loves you better' story. Or, the 'my brother and sister are super educated' story. Or my personal favorite, 'everybody hates Jacob because he gave me the good life' story. Which one?"

Mychal made an exaggerated silly face, "All of them."

"Wow and what did Ma do?"

"Set it off by her usual larger than needed reactions. You should have seen her 'Oh Mychal this place is so great'. It was followed by 'Your sister hooked a nice guy' with undertones of Jacob is a loser. And of course Richard was just being the nice guy that he is. He didn't know how Ma would turn the simplest stuff into something that made Riley feel like her own self-described failure. And I did not tell him because I didn't want him to change who he is for their foolishness."

Reese shook his head, "I knew it was something. All three came back saying Richard was perfect for you and that you had never been happier. But Riley was sullen. It was like she could not be happy for herself and happy for you at the same time."

She rolled her eyes, "That's just stupid because her happiness should not be based on other peoples' lives."

"I know. I know. I think your wedding made her think about her own future with Jake."

"Then she needs to tell him to take the damn deal."

Reese covered her hand in assurance, "Believe me, she thinks about nothing else. According to Max, it's not just the time but the money as well. She is looking at an uncertain future."

"Reese, please. Richard and I agreed to let her stay in Ma's house if she would just pay the taxes and upkeep until she got on her feet financially. You got her a job and Max plans to have their taxes redone to set up a payment schedule for her. With that structure in place, parts of her future should not be that uncertain."

Reese thought for a minute, "So all that in addition to Jake not getting any serious time?"

"Yes, nobody but Riley cares how it gets done. She is looking at everything as a handout, not as family coming together to support her."

"I understand everything now," was all he could say before Gwen and Max came to the table.

The next day started out lounging by the pool. Everybody slept in before slowly making their way down to the pool. Mychal had a breakfast of fruits, tarts, crepes and toasted baguettes. Susanna and Javier joined the crowd for breakfast then departed for their day.

Richard had a day of sightseeing planned for the group. Mychal's family loaded into his SUV and headed out for the city. After their day of city sights, Richard threw a cookout by the pool and invited Ruby and Luis, Susanna and Javier, Tony and Yadira and Uncle Rico. The food, conversation, and drinks flowed into the late hours. Mychal put Carrigan to bed and came back to enjoy her family. Slowly the party dissipated and after hours of trying to stay awake, Mychal called it a night, leaving Reese, Max and Richard engaged in a deep conversation.

The christening of Carrigan Alejandra Iban Garçia-Torrés was more of a celebration than a religious event. The priest from Richard's childhood church dedicated her in his church office with just close family and godparents in attendance. When the service was over, they changed plans and went back to the house. Once there, Mychal immediately noted the activity.

"What is all this?"

Richard and Max exchanged looks and Max said, "We godparents got together to give Carrigan an early birthday party. It was Susanna's idea. She wanted us all to be here."

Mychal was touched by such thoughtfulness. Her eyes clouded with tears while saying thank you.

Reese chimed in, "Quit with the water works or you'll wash out this party."

The truck erupted in laughter.

Carrigan's birthday party had everything that Mychal probably would not have had if she was planning it, starting with the petting zoo and bounce house. There were people everywhere, friends, family, teenagers, little kids, and elderly aunts and uncles. The day wore into night seeing the elderly and parents with younger children trickle out. When Mychal put the baby down for the night, she fell asleep on the daybed in her room.

"Mychal," someone was calling her name and shaking her, "are you okay?"

When the fog cleared Mychal recognized Gwen and Yvonne. She sat up an asked, "How long have I been asleep? What time is it?"

Gwen sat beside her and Yvonne sat on the ottoman. "You've been gone maybe an hour?"

"Where's Richard?"

Gwen laughed, "He and your

remaining male guest are watching a polo match. I think the remaining wives are outside with their kids. When Susanna left, we didn't know anybody, so we came to find you."

Mychal smiled, "I'm glad you came. Up here, and to visit."

"When Reese said let's visit my sister and her husband in Spain, I think my bag was packed before he could finish the sentence. Your wedding was so beautiful. I really wished we could have been there."

"Yvonne, I wished everyone could come and I hated it was right in the middle of your vacation." She sighed, "But everything happened so fast. One minute I am living a dream, and the next I was moving out. Richard came and fought to get me back, even as I resolved to raise Carrigan by myself, like everything else I have done."

Gwen grinned, "Oh, I can believe

that. He is definitely a quiet storm. But I can see he loves you. I am happy that you found that special someone. Max has always worried about you being alone. Now he talks to Richard like a brother. He can finally focus on other things."

Mychal caught that last statement, "Like what?"

"We are going to expand the family."

Yvonne and Mychal exchanged looks. Yvonne spoke first, "Is there something we need to know? Like are you expecting now?"

"We are trying. Carrigan made Max want a girl."

"Well congratulations."

"Not yet. Max wants to have the Riley drama behind us, but that may take forever. If we are going to do this, we need to get moving. I'm no spring chicken."

"I know what you mean. Reese wants to move to White Plains or Mount Vernon, but he wants to make sure Riley is stable."

Mychal huffed, "She has Ma's house and Ma lives twenty minutes away. I am so tired of the millstone of other people's problems around my neck. Riley, Jacob, Richard's work, I can't wait for all that shi-, I mean stuff to be over."

Gwen looked confused, "I thought Max said everything ended when Richard's ex died. Is there something else?"

"Richard, Tony and Evan seem to think so, but he is keeping whatever else super low key. He wants to have a normal life aside from the security and all. If it was over, the security would be gone."

Yvonne chuckled, "Yeah, Iroh is more than a family friend. I made him as bodyguard material at the airport."

Mychal smiled, "I forgot you did

security before moving to New York."

"He's still a good guy and he loves that little girl. Did you see him today with the baby goats and Carrigan? It was clear he hated the smell, but was right there when she wanted to see them."

"When he picked up Ma and Riley, she was like 'Don't get no ideas Riley," Mychal imitated her mother's raspy voice.

"I know she was sour," Yvonne rolled her eyes. "I think that is the real problem concerning Jake taking the deal. If the situation involved anybody else but you, he would have copped a plea deal with her blessing because his punk ass can't handle prison. But because it *is* you offering to help and you being a witness versus being implicated, in her eyes you got to walk away free."

"I know and for those very reasons, I let Richard and Max deal with her. Although she has changed, there is some of the old Riley still beneath the surface."

"Honey, honey, where are you?" Reese was calling from the stairs.

Yvonne was up and out the door, hushing him before he could wake the baby. She poked her head in the room and motioned for the other two to come.

Gwen was worried, "What is it? Is everything at home okay?"

Reese was out of breath but managed, "Max and Richard are on the phone with Riley. She thinks Jake is going to take the plea deal."

13
Letters and Presents

The rest of the time Mychal's family was in Spain was jubilant thanks to the news about Jacob. Even their usually sad departure was upbeat. All agreed the dark cloud over their family was gone. Returning home from the airport, Mychal and Richard celebrated by finishing leftovers along with a celebratory bottle of champagne then taking a family nap. They were tired from the visit and so was Carrigan. When she woke up, Mychal took her in the pool to play. Richard fixed dinner and after watching some television, they were ready for bed, still tired from the weekend. He bathed the baby while she showered and pumped milk. Since Carrigan's little teeth had come in, Mychal's breasts were sensitive from nursing her. Mychal was relying on the pump more and more. She gave Richard a bottle and took the others downstairs to the refrigerator. She let the dog out while downstairs. When Mychal came upstairs Richard was in the bed on the phone. Mychal slid into bed beside him.

"That was Max. They are home."

"Good," she went to kiss him.

Instead Richard grabbed his wife in a tight hug and let out a slow breath. "It is finally over. I feel that weight gone off my chest."

"I know. I never knew how tiring worrying could be and then there was Riley and Jacob."

"I think I am working from home tomorrow. That way I can sleep in. Do you mind getting up with her in the morning?"

"No, I'll be up anyway. I am working on an idea to present to the department chair for the fall semester." She noticed Richard was completely naked except for the gold chain around his neck she gave him as a birthday gift.

"Thanks Bella because tonight we are celebrating as well," he gave her a passionate kiss that was only the beginning of their night.

When Richard went to work Thursday, he had more than a plan, he had a mission. He stopped by Tony's office where he found his brother at his desk staring into space. Tony noticed Richard and gave him a weak smile.

"What's wrong?" Richard knew his brother.

Tony sighed and said nothing at first. Then he said, "I am in love with Yadira."

Richard raised an eyebrow but did not respond to the subject that Tony obviously needed to talk about.

"This feels different. It's great but I . . . I . . . I don't know how I am supposed to feel."

"Sounds like you might be falling in love," his brother smiled. "It's great, but at the same time it is overwhelming and scary. Think of it as your walk down the hill just became a run. Now you are afraid that you are going too fast and might hurt yourself."

"Exactly," Tony deflated and slumped back in his chair.

"When did you realize all of this?"

"At Carrigan's party. I saw Yadira with the family and everything seemed so natural. I told her that I loved her and could imagine a life like that for us. You know what I mean, holidays, family birthdays and other events."

"Wow," Richard was pleasantly surprised, "and she said?"

"She wants the same but no kids right now. She wants to make sure we can make it. She also wants to make sure my old ways are out of my system." When Richard gave him a confused look, Tony continued, "Sometimes we go out and will see one of my old girlfriends. That has happened a few times and Yadira is a bit uneasy now.

"A few times?"

"Like thirty-four," Tony gave Richard a pained smile, who returned it with a 'I told you' look. "I know, okay. You have been telling me forever to clean up my image. That is not the image I really wanted. You told me I was being a *canella* and it would catch up with me. I get it. But that was before her. Before I realized that all of the women and parties meant nothing. Before I knew the love of one person was enough."

"So now what?"

"I'm going to buy a ring and ask her to marry me."

"Whoa," Richard put his hand in the stop position. "You are running down the hill again. You just said your past makes her nervous, so a new ring will make things better? Tony, this plan- "

"Well, what do you suggest?" his brother interrupted, frustrated. "You did it and Mychal married you. I mean she was pregnant, but even I knew you two were going to be together, especially after that night Demitri came to tell you everything she knew about Mychal."

"What? How did you think that we were going to be together? You were the one who drove her to Ruby's house." Richard was stunned at his brother's admission.

"Exactly. I knew you needed space. That blowup was minor drama compared to some of my own breakups. Hell it was mild compared to your last breakup with Demitri and Mychal was pregnant with the child you always wanted. Let's face it, you wanted to be a father when we had a father."

Richard sighed as Tony's truth soaked in, "But Papa was overwhelmed with Mama. I just wanted to help."

Tony laughed, "Who kept me out of trouble when our hermana had recitals? You. Who read to me and taught me how to throw an American football? You. Who checked my homework, took me to practices and showed up to games? Shall I keep going?"

"No."

"Right, because you were destine to be someone's good father. We knew that you would be a great pseudo single dad if you ended up with Demitri. She was so selfish, that if she gave you a child, you would be the sole caregiver. Me and Susanna were so glad when the two of you broke up permanently. And when you started to be interested in Mychal, we were secretly planning to do everything to make it work. Remember I was her partner in crime when we went out on that weird date."

"I remember because Mychal had on the shortest dress in the history of the country." Richard's mind drifted to that night when he first made love to his wife.

"Part of the plan that obviously worked. In short order you moved into her room. Look at you now smiling just thinking about it," Tony teased his older brother. "So after your first real major fight, I knew it was not the end of your relationship. That and she told me how much she loved you all the way there. She explained her situation at home, how she was not trying to trap you, how she never loved anybody the way she loved you, and how she wanted a future with you, just not in the order it was going."

"So why did you let me suffer? You could have shared that information instead of letting me drag through those weeks until she came back."

"No. You two needed to work things out. Susanna and I were just waiting for the good news."

"Thanks for the trip down memory lane, but back to you now. Follow your own previous example. Give her room to have her feelings. As she works through them, support her while showing her the genuine love you two share. That will build her trust. Make her feel like she is the only one that you want to build a future with before you show up with a ring." A silence hung in the room after Richard's last comment.

"So how about I buy a house and move her in?"

"Running down the hill again, but

better," Richard shook his head. "Why don't you talk to her? If you think moving in together will build trust, you might be right. Nothing like seeing if you two have what it takes before saying I do."

Tony liked the idea, "True. Knowing Yadira, it will take a minute to get her to buy into this idea. Hopefully she will, and I will move out of the apartment by the end of the year."

"Sounds like a good plan, "Richard rose to leave. "Wait *Hermano*, something happened while you were out. Demitri's lawyer had a letter delivered on Monday."

"What does it say?"

Tony gave him a comical look, "I don't know. I wanted to wait until you came back to work to open it."

"But you could have called me."

"I know, but you and Mychal were so happy her brother-in-law took the plea

313

deal. I was not going to rain on your happiness."

Richard smiled, "Thanks *hermano*. When Evan gets here, we will open it together."

When Evan arrived, the three sat in Tony's office talking, but also waiting for the other to take the initiative to open the letter. Evan joked, "It's not a bomb is it?"

"No, the lawyer hand delivered it Monday."

Richard made the comment, "Then it is not laced with arsenic."

The three men looked at each other.

"Just give me the damn letter," Evan snatched up the letter and opened it. The handwriting was thin and elegant, a mere reflection of the author.

He read aloud,

"Dear Tony, I hope all is well when

this letter reaches you, because if you are receiving this letter I am long gone. I wanted to thank you for your kindness even after I almost took your life. Your visit let me know I was not totally unredeemable. I feel now that I need to confess a few things and it is up to you to share that information if you choose. Let me start by saying I was the one who destroyed Richard's car. Yes, it was petty but also therapeutic; I am ashamed to admit. One day I was in the garage and saw the Nigerian breaking into Richard's car. I surprised him, which is how I got the upper hand. That is when I first heard the name Amato Delossantos. He said tell Mr. Delossantos that he was planning something that would make the company lose enough money to shut down or be sold. I told him I did not care and threaten his life if I ever saw him again or he interfered in my plans.

Our paths never crossed again, but I did meet Delossantos in person. I had just moved in with Rafael and was running the house. His sister called their uncle and he came for a social visit slash interrogation. Even at his age, he was a shrewd and dominating presence. I did not recognize how dangerous he was as I was consumed by my own hate. He let on that he was aware of my activities. I responded by warning him to stay out of my way. He laughed at me like I was some silly child and said I had no clue what was really going on. Delossantos countered with his own warning that if his nephew got hurt in my schemes, that I would regret such an action. I ignored his polite tête-à-tête because all I wanted was Richard to pay for breaking my heart.

After Richard came to visit me in jail, I realized how I left the door open for that woman to walk into my relationship- "

"That *perra loca!*" Richard interrupted. Both Tony and Evan gave him a dirty look. "Sorry, but you know she was."

Evan continued to read, "-*and away with the best thing in my life. The way he looked at me was as if I was a monster. Here was the love of my life pointing out how he and many others almost died because of me. That is when I realized how my pursuit of vengeance really affected the one I loved. I wanted to apologize which I knew would not fix any of the events, but would let Richard know I had accepted my part in what happened. Of course, he would not see me again, which is why I was glad the lawyer got you to come Tony.*

When you told me the addict was dead and the conversation you had with a mysterious Nigerian, I knew something was happening to the people who knew Amato's plans to obtain Richard's company. I told my lawyer to cut a deal and move me if he could. I was moved to the psychiatric wing of the prison, which is where I am writing from today. But if you are reading this letter, Amato Delossantos has made good on his promise to make me pay the ultimate price for my actions.

Please guard yourselves against this man and perhaps Rafael. I am not sure how much he knew about his uncle's plans for your family. He is not to be trusted. I wish you, Susanna and most of all, Richard the best. I hope you will one day find forgiveness in your heart. I was never a monster, just my own worst enemy.

Demitri Salvadore Salvos

The room was quiet for a moment. Tony spoke first, "What do we do with this new piece of information? Go to the authorities?"

Evan replied, "This is a letter from a dead person accusing a foreign business mogul of her death. Other than her accusations, there is no proof linking the two events and we will look suspicious with this letter."

"But, she did give us the last piece of the puzzle, by confirming what the Nigerian said about why the owner of the Ares corporation was trying to sabotage the company." Tony turned to Richard, "What are you thinking?"

"I have no idea what to think. For now, we need to keep the letter to ourselves. Evan, no sharing with your detective girlfriend."

"Come on *jefé.*"

"I need to think." Richard got up to leave, "If you need me call my cell."

After telling Morcheeba he would be working from home, Richard picked up lunch and headed to the cemetery. En route he sent Mychal a text that he was visiting his parents and would call her later. Her response was what was wrong. He replied that he needed to think and loved her. He spent the next few hours working on two things: his emotions and a plan.

Carrigan's first birthday was emotional for Mychal. She took her first solo steps following the dog. Her parents smiled at each other and Richard videoed some of the milestone with his phone. Her birthday dinner was her favorite of minced chicken, chilled peeled cucumber halves for her gums and vanilla pudding. She babbled to her numerous family members via video link. Mychal waited to call her sister last, dreading the anticipated drama.

To the contrary, her sister was surprisingly pleasant. She was excited to see Carrigan and happy to talk with her sister. Mychal was guarded but tried to return her sister's good demeanor. She was glad when the baby got fussy and she had to call for Richard. He came in looking concerned.

"Can you talk with Riley while I change her?" Mychal was getting up before he could even answer. Once in Carrigan's room, Mychal did change her but took extra-long hoping Richard would stay on the phone for the rest of the call. She played with the tired infant then put away folded clothes. Anything to keep from going back in the room.

"*Bella*, your sister wanted to say goodbye," Richard called. Mychal rolled her eyes but went back into the room to get this painful conversation over with.

When she walked back in the room Riley said from the screen, "There's auntie's girl."

Mychal managed a smile. Richard got up to take the baby, "Say goodnight auntie. She has to tell mommy her good news."

Mychal sat down, "Good news?"

Riley smiled, "Yeah sis. Jake took the deal and it was not so bad. The fine was a little over five hundred thousand but Richard said you would forgo your restitution to help out."

"Oh he did?"

"Yes, and he suggested some place to apply to get a better job. The guy who owns the company went to college with him in Miami. But the best part is the time. Jake got ten years but the judge gave him double time served. He has to serve eighty percent of his time but that can be done as community service with monitored supervision. So, he will be out in a little less than three years. One of the downsides is he can't ever apply for federal loans and his investor license has been revoked." Riley took a breath, "It is a lot, but at least we can still have a life together."

"Wow," was all Mychal could manage.

"But we still might need a place to stay after he gets out. I was wondering if you could give us maybe a year or two after he gets out to get on our feet."

"Sure. Whatever."

Riley looked relieved, "Thanks sis. I knew you would understand. Well I got to run since I promised Ma I would drive her to this thing for her senior club. I love you guys."

"Love you too," Mychal signed off. Without missing a beat, she went looking for Richard. She found him in his office on a call.

"Okay Evan, go to phase two. Make sure I get that key. Thanks again and good night." Mychal was just waiting. He hung up and asked, "Your sister seems happy, are you?"

"Maybe if I knew what was really going on."

"What do you mean? You do know what's going on. Her husband took the deal and got off light. Everybody is happy. Right?"

She gave Richard an annoyed look, "I guess I misheard something about forgoing the restitution. Don't play with me, just spill it."

Based on his wife's mannerisms, she was poised to fight; so he came clean. "When Max and Reese were here, we discussed the ways that the whole situation could play out. One of the possibilities was that the federal prosecutor could still see you as an accomplice. Long before he started working on Riley's taxes, Max was working on yours. He found a paper trail where you reported a contribution to Jacob's company as a partner. This was filed twice on your taxes with no profit from the business to you. That information proved you were a victim as well."

"That is what I have been saying from day one."

"I know *Bella*, but the people to convince were the judge and prosecutor. That was Max's main goal, while his secondary was to give Riley a chance for a life after this situation. He worked with Jacob's attorney after they received the initial plea deal to counter with one of their own to reduce the time. When Max called about the restitution to all injured parties, meaning you, I told him to ask the judge if what he would have been fined to pay you could be credited to reduce his overall amount. Then Uncle Rico, as your representative, had to confer that decision with the judge and prosecutor. It helped a little considering his overall sentence was fair. He got double credit for his days in jail and the fine was double the amount he defrauded the government."

She huffed, "Like he doubled my suffering and worry over a lie."

Richard got up and hugged her. Her body was stiff with anger. He kissed her forehead. "*Bella*, his greed created a situation that hurt everyone, including his own wife. That in turn aggravated the tense relationship between you and your sister and brothers. You have no idea of the emotional things Riley has said to your mother and your brothers on a daily basis. They purposely kept that from you knowing someone tried to kill you and that you were adjusting to motherhood."

"But not you?"

"No, because I have no history with your family and am new to the whole situation. In essence I am looking at everything through an impartial lens. Max always understood my viewpoints and once I explained them to Reese, he was on board. We all wanted to resolve everything for our families but especially you by Carrigan's birthday. Even Uncle Rico sent supporting information from international cases to help Jacob's attorney."

Mychal's heart softened, dissolving her anger. Richard's efforts to spearhead a campaign to fix decades of dysfunction in her family were beyond amazing. She hugged him tighter and told him so,

"Thank you for that amazing gift. I love you."

"I love you more. Now can we celebrate?" he was already caressing her thighs.

"Like it's the fourth of July," she led the way to their bedroom.

As her birthday approached Mychal had a notion to give Richard a present on her special day. He had been preoccupied with something at work since the family's visit, so she brought him lunch for her birthday.

"I thought I was taking you out," Richard was surprised.

"You still can. I just wanted to make sure you ate lunch today," she smiled. "You have been engrossed in work lately."

"I know. I am just tying up some loose ends before we expand the company in new areas."

"Tell me your ideas of what you have planned," she was genuinely interested to know. For the next hour, Richard talked about expanding the company to include a trucking division and possibly multiple partnerships, a few with naval apprentice schools. Richard was moving slowly on the expansion because he was conflicted between honoring his father's original ideas and moving the company in a more progressive direction. At the end of lunch she was again blown away with her husband's business acuity. As she got ready to leave, Mychal kissed Richard and promised to see him at home early. When she left his office, she stopped by Morcheeba's desk to leave him a present that he would get at the end of the day.

Mychal was outside playing with their daughter and the dog when Richard came home. He came outside, present in hand. He took her in his arms to deliver a passionate kiss.

She broke their kiss to say, "You got my present I see."

"I did and this time I want a boy."

She smiled at her clever idea of her pregnancy test as his gift, "I just want a healthy baby."

"Can I request two boys?" Richard winked. He picked up Carrigan, "How about you? Don't you want two brothers?'

Carrigan gave her dad a funny face and said her new favorite word, "No."

Richard tightly hugged his girls. Everything he had done up to this point was to ensure the safety of his now expanding family. The chapter in his life involving harming them and the company was closed. Mychal's problems back in the States were over with her family on the way to healing old wounds. Now they were finally looking toward a promising future. Richard closed his eyes and slowly exhaled, enjoying the serenity after their storm.

Epilogue

Richard sat at the bar in a posh hotel in Greece nursing a neat scotch. He watched the dignified gentleman sitting by the window with his after dinner coffee. He was a petite man by standards, but his leathered face and ultra-neat appearance gave off the air of an important man. Dismissing his threatening anger, Richard paid for his drink with money under the glass. He made his way to that table by the window and quietly sat down. "Tell your bodyguard at the station by the kitchen and the bartender that you are fine. We are just going to have a civil conversation and I do not need any interruptions."

The elderly gentleman gave Richard a steely, piercing look but complied by signaling his security.

"Thank you sir." Richard tapped the window twice, his own signal. "That young man in the office across the street with a custom sniper rifle trained to protect me can now enjoy the rest of his night."

The elderly gentleman raised an eyebrow, "A civil conversation you say?"

"Of course. We both know violence is such a roguish method of handling business. I find a cultured gentleman's ways and words are much more effective means," Richard gave Amato Delossantos a sly smile, knowing his words had hidden meanings for them both.

When the other man said nothing, Richard leaned forward and extracted the envelope he had hidden in the small of his back. He slid it over to the elderly man who opened it and sifted through the photos of himself over the past six months, his children, grandchildren, nieces, nephews, wife and mistresses.

"This is the end of us," Richard spoke as the man looked at the duplicates of police photos of the dead addict, Nigerian, and Demitri. As he viewed the copy of Demitri's letter, Richard noticed a slight tremor in the older man's hand.

Amato asked, "What is this, some sort of extortion attempt or blackmail?"

"Extortion and blackmail? Oh no. This is simply the end of any interaction between us. Ever. With a gentleman's word, I never want to see you again, even when you visit your nephew. Everything concerning my family, my business, and you is done. We both know that is the preferred way to conduct business," Richard extended his hand.

Amato did not shake his hand. But instead sat back, eyes blazing with loathing.

"I see," Richard retracted his hand to reach inside his jacket to produce a black velvet box. He slid it over within the other man's reach. "We will do this like everything else, the hard way. I will start with the fact that you do not like tan lines. So, whenever you are home, you swim naked and sometimes spend hours sunbathing, usually napping. The only thing you wear are the necklace your sister, Rafael's mother gave you and your father's ring that was passed down from his father. Three weeks ago, that ring went missing. You turned your house upside down looking for it. You had your staff's quarters gone through and you even searched the home of your latest mistress. The short twenty-year-old with the breast job you paid for. She is about the same age as Altagraçia, your granddaughter that lives in England, right? Your office was searched and you upset a great many people with your accusations of theft."

Delossantos turned dark with rage, "You have gone too far!"

"You put my entire family in danger in some twisted scheme to ruin my name and possibly force me to sell my birthright in hopes to gain control of my company. And now, *you* are telling *me* what is going too far?" Richard could not even be angry because the other man's warped irony was almost comical, "Seriously?"

The elderly gentleman raised an eyebrow in touché.

He put his hand out again and said five words, all humor gone, "Your word it is over."

"Are these the only copies?"

"Do not give me your word and you will find out."

Delossantos smirked, "I heard that you were a calculating bastard of a business man but I never thought you had this move in you. Well played. You turned out to be quite the adversary. For that you have earned my respect and my word."

They shook hands.

"Good bye Roman Ricardo Garçia-Torrés. While you are heir of Rohas and Alejandra Garçia-Torrés, you are nothing like them. *Epaíschynto.* I hope to never cross paths with you again."

"You will not. Under the ring are my copies of the keys to everything you own, business and personal." Richard stood up and dug in his pants pocket. He threw a single key on top of the pile of photographs, "That is the key to the desk in your home office. Good bye Amato Delossantos."

Richard walked out of the restaurant struggling to contain his emotions. He walked down the street mind working. For what seemed like an eternity, he was always on the brink of fear, anger, panic, and fatigue. At that very moment freedom felt strangely surreal.

"*Jefé*, let's go," Evan was waiting by the curb a block away in a black Mercedes sedan.

On the chartered jet ride home, he talked to Uncle Rico then Max while Evan

337

slept. After checking on his wife, pregnant with twin boys, and daughter, he settled in for the rest of the flight. Richard closed his eyes and exhaled. For the first time in a lifetime he was truly at peace.

SE ACABÓ

ABOUT THE AUTHOR

Sean Scott Kerns currently lives in the Hampton Roads area of Virginia. Sean's previous works have been published in the *Rhapsody in Black* magazine since the early 1990s. Her passions include travel and martial arts. The Foreign Engagement is the follow up book to Sean's first novel The Foreign Exchange. The Foreign Endgame completes the Foreign Exchange trilogy. She is currently in talks to begin a series of novelettes about different character within the series.

Check out her website at

www.seanscottkerns.com